WILLOW LANDING

by CHRISTINE GOVAN

Illustrated by Mary Stevens

Nell was used to being in trouble because of her cats, but when Natchez, the big battle-scarred tom she loved because no one else did, bit off the head of Rena's frizzly chicken, Rena's grief at the loss of her pet was almost more than Nell could bear. The queer-looking little chicken "with its feathers all turned backward" would have to be replaced, but where could Nell find another? Even with the help of her lively cousins, all her efforts to beg, buy, and finally "borrow" a frizzly were merely frustrating failures. And in the end, it was only after the most humiliating disgrace that impulsive, lovable Nell redeemed herself and found a solution to her problems.

The way of life in the dusty little one-street town along the Mississippi River that Mrs. Govan has re-created so vividly in these pages is gone forever now, but young readers everywhere will recognize themselves in the children of this engaging family story. Its warmth and mood are delightfully reflected in Mary Stevens' turn-of-the-century drawings.

WILLOW LANDING

By the same author
The Year the River Froze

WILLOW LANDING

by CHRISTINE GOVAN

Illustrated by Mary Stevens

THE WORLD PUBLISHING COMPANY

CLEVELAND AND NEW YORK

PUBLISHED BY The World Publishing Company

2231 West 110th Street, Cleveland 2, Ohio

PUBLISHED SIMULTANEOUSLY IN CANADA BY

Nelson, Foster & Scott Ltd.

Library of Congress Catalog Card Number: 61-9086

FIRST EDITION

The folk song on page 28 is reprinted from Ben Lucien Burman's book *Big River to Cross* with permission of the author.

HC261

For Jane—this shadow of a memory,
and for the real Nell wherever she may be

Contents

5

WILLOW LANDING

"The Showboat's Coming!"

It was cool inside the house, for in all the rooms the shutters at the windows—which reached from ceiling to floor—were drawn against the sun. In the big center hall with doors that opened wide at both ends, there was even a faint breeze stirring. At the rear of the hall was a latticed porch shaded with morning-glory vines. Nelly's grandmother, her mother, and her two aunts were sitting there now. Nelly could hear them laughing and talking as they sewed.

That was Aunt Cara laughing now. Her husband, Uncle Doctor, said that Aunt Cara's laugh sounded like water pouring out of a jug. It did have a sort of gurgle to it, and it nearly always made any-

9

body who heard it laugh, too. But Nelly didn't laugh. She didn't even smile. Her face was as dark as a thundercloud, and her eyes were as sad as a lost hound dog's.

It was not only *not* cool on the front steps where she sat, it was hot as Tophet. It was so hot that she could not keep her bare feet still on the wooden steps for very long. Even the big pool of shade that the pecan tree by the porch spread over the yard and steps, had not kept the heat from sinking into everything.

In the dusty bare spot under the chinaberry tree lay a striped mother cat and her four half-grown kittens. The kittens rolled and played with each other's tails while the mother cat lay and looked at them proudly. Every now and then she or her kittens would stop and scratch so hard you wondered the fur did not fly off them. And every time they did this Nelly looked impatiently next door to see if her two cousins were coming.

"For the last time," Nelly's mother had said just a few minutes before, "I am telling you to do something about the fleas on your cats. If you don't, I'll have to ask Uncle Doctor to do something about them."

This had a dreadful sound. Did her mother mean that Uncle Doctor would take the cats far out into the country in his buggy and give them to some farmer for barn cats, or did she mean that he would "put them to sleep," as he had done with his hound dog when it got too old to eat? Nelly shuddered at the thought of either of these happening to her beloved pets.

She had sent her six-year-old cousin Benjy to ask Callie and Rose to come over and help her give the cats a bath with naphtha soap. Rena, who ruled over the kitchen, had told her that naphtha soap would kill the fleas and as Nelly knew no other way to do it, she was anxious to try it.

Benjy, who was Callie's little brother, came back and said they'd be over as soon as Rose was dressed. He was almost six but a crybaby and poor company, Nelly felt. He would be no help in washing the cats, but he could run errands.

All he had done all morning was to put his finger in his mouth and wiggle his loose front tooth. Nelly had offered to pull it for him, but he was afraid. His face had clouded up and he had started to sniffle, so she'd just given him a punch and refused to have anything else to do with him.

"I wish Callie'd come on without Rose," muttered Nelly. "Rose isn't going to be any help, anyway."

Rose did not like to touch cats. She was afraid of getting dirty. Rose never got dirty. The cousins could play all morning and, as Nelly's mother pointed out, Rose would still come home looking as sweet as the flower she had been named for.

"And that Callie," old Rena would say. "She's as sweet as a calla lily. She don't *look* dirty, even when she is!" It was true. Callie, with her clear dark eyes and fair hair, always looked as white and pure as a lily even when she had on a dirty frock and her bare feet were muddy or gray with dust.

But Nelly! Nelly always came home with a dirty face, scratches, a torn or muddy dress. Nelly's curly hair blew into witch locks, and if anybody got a bruise or a cut during one of their daily explorations, it was Nelly. Not even the boys could get into so much trouble.

Callie and Rose were Nelly's first cousins. Their mothers were sisters. But Callie's father and Rose's father were brothers as well, so Callie and Rose were *double* first cousins. Whenever the girls had a quarrel—which was not often—Callie and Rose sided against Nelly.

"Because you see," Rose would explain, "we

are double first cousins; but your papa wasn't kin to any of us. Even Missmamma isn't your real grandmother. She's our papas' mamma."

This always made Nelly feel a little lonely and left out. But there was nothing she could say to it, for it was a fact.

Sometimes Callie would point out that not only was Nelly's father no kin to them, but he was *almost a Northerner,* which was worse! He had come from upstate Kentucky. He was probably a Yankee.

"He was not a Yankee!" Nelly would cry when Callie teased her. "Captain Tom P. Leathers was from Kentucky, and *he* wasn't a Yankee."

Even Callie knew that Captain Leathers had been the best steamboat captain on the Mississippi in his time. He had lived at Natchez and been captain of the famous steamboat of that name. Nobody could accuse him of being a Yankee, so Rose would think up some other way to tease Nelly and add her bit to Callie's.

"I always thought your papa was a Yankee," she would say. "Nobody ever said he *wasn't.* Besides, he might just have been visiting in Kentucky when Aunt Fanny met him."

Poor Nelly! She had been born just after her father died and had never seen him, so she found it hard to defend him. She could only cry with rage and say that he must have been all right or her mother would not have married him. At this, Rose would simply look superior and say nothing—as if she could say plenty if she wanted to—and Callie would say, "Hm-mm!"

Nelly never told her mother or her aunts about this teasing. Nobody likes a tattletale. Besides, suppose they were right. It was better not to know.

After Nelly was born her mother had come home to live near her two sisters. She and Nelly lived in the house beneath the pecan tree. Callie lived next door with her two brothers, her mother, and her father, who was a doctor. In the house beyond Callie's lived Rose and her mother and father, who was called Judge because he was a lawyer; and with them lived Missmamma.

It was lots of fun to have the cousins to play with, especially as there were not many other children in the small town of Willow Landing, Mississippi. And Nelly liked being called one of the "Doctor's children," because she loved her jolly doctor-uncle.

Most of the time the three girls were happy and busy. Only occasionally Callie and Rose got tired of Nelly's cats.

Any stray or sick cat could find a home with

Nelly. There were eight of them now that Memphis Belle had kittens. Nelly loved them even more than she loved the great steamboats that went up and down the river, blowing their mournful whistles and churning the brown water into white foam. All the cats were named for steamboats. There was Natchez and River Queen and Rosalie and Memphis Belle. Sometimes there was a Robert E. Lee and once when Nelly ran out of steamboat names, she called a fierce old tom with one eye Captain Tom P. Leathers for the great river captain.

Just that morning Callie's father, Uncle Doctor, had looked at Memphis Belle's kittens and said, "These are so runty I think you'll have to name 'em after shanty boats." He picked one up and held it in the palm of his hand. "Not much bigger than a boll weevil," he said. "You ought to call this one Goober. It's the same shape at both ends, like a goober shell."

Name my lovely kitten after a peanut? thought Nelly, taking the kitten away from him indignantly. It *was* the same shape at both ends now, but that was just because kittens always have little round heads and round ears so small they are almost hidden in their fur. The kitten had a lovely white face and a nose as pink as a rosebud.

I'm going to name her the prettiest name of all,

Nelly said to herself. I'm going to call her Magnolia Queen.

"My tooth hurts," whined Benjy.

"Of course it does. You keep wiggling it, and you make the gum sore," said Nelly. "If you weren't such a baby, you'd let me pull it. I could tie a thread around it and tie the other end to the doorknob. Then I'd slam the door and zip!—it'd be out before you knew it. It's so quick you can't feel it. I swear you can't. I've had dozens pulled that way."

Benjy looked both hopeful and scared.

"It won't really hurt?" he asked, looking a little pale.

"You won't even know it," declared Nelly, who welcomed the idea of having something to do. "Come on, I'll get some thread from Mamma."

She took the little boy's hand, and the two of them went across the porch into the cool, dim hall.

"Don't tell 'em you're gonna pull my tooth," begged Benjy.

"I won't," said Nelly. She knew Benjy wanted a chance to back out if his courage failed him. There was no use having the family on the scene if he was going to be a coward, after all. "I'll just ask Mamma for a piece of thread. You stay here!"

It was cool and shady on the back porch, for the

sun had not yet reached that side of the house. The pale light fell in pretty patterns across the four ladies who sat there sewing.

Nelly's mother had very dark hair. She wore a white dress with pink ribbons at the short sleeves and neck of the dress. She looked up as Nelly came out on the porch and raised her eyebrows. She did not ask about the cats. Apparently she had said her last word on *that* subject!

"May I have a long piece of thread?" asked Nelly.

"What color?" asked her mother.

"It doesn't matter." Nelly hoped that her mother wouldn't ask her what it was for.

"My, it's hot!" exclaimed Missmamma. "Isn't the ice boat due this afternoon?"

"Yes, it is," said Aunt Rosalie, biting off a bit of pink thread. "We'll get some extra and make some lemonade."

"Here." Nelly's mother wrapped a long piece of white thread around her fingers into a little skein.

"Thank you," said Nelly, hurrying back into the hall. She felt a little cheered. She was going to pull Benjy's tooth, and the ice boat from Greenville was coming that afternoon. Any boat's arrival was fun, but the ice boat was sort of special. They always went down to the levee and watched the men unload the great blocks of ice packed deep in sawdust in the hold. Sometimes they followed the wagons to the ice house and stood around to grab any chips that might break off when the men cut chunks of ice for customers. Then they rode home on the wagon that Big Asa drove down to the ice house when he got ice for all three of their families. When Asa wasn't looking, they put their bare feet on the cold blocks or even sat on them as long as they could stand the freezing cold.

Benjy was waiting for Nelly in the hall, looking quite terrified now. His face was so white that even in shadow his freckles stood out like the spots on a guinea egg. As Nelly came close to him his blue eyes filled with tears.

"Great snortin' alligators!" cried Nelly. "I'm not gonna *hang* you! Hold still. I've got to tie it tight around the tooth. It's so . . . slippery. . . . Oh, darn! It slipped off. Wait a minute. I think . . . I've got it . . . this time. There!"

After a short struggle with the damp thread and Benjy's trembling lip she had it tied. Nelly gave it a gentle pull to see if it would hold, and Benjy moaned.

"Now I'll tie it to the door handle. Come on,"

she said, moving toward the parlor door. Benjy, grabbing the string, followed nervously. She was just reaching for the doorknob when Rose and Callie came running up the front steps.

"Nell! Nell! Guess what?" cried Rose. "Look! It'll be here tomorrow!"

"I can't wait!" shrieked Callie, waving a sheet of pink paper in Nelly's face.

"Look!" Rose cried again. "Willy Steamboat is givin' 'em out. Oh, I can't wait either!"

Forgetting all about Benjy, Nell reached for the paper. There was a sharp howl behind her, and she looked around to see him holding a hand to his mouth. At the end of the thread hung a small bloody tooth.

"Oh, Benjy! I forgot. But your tooth's out. It didn't hurt, now did it? Oh, don't start bellerin'!"

Benjy swallowed a sob. He stared at his tooth. Then he put his tongue in the gap where his tooth had been, and a look of wonder and relief came over his face. He picked up the thread and wandered out the front door. The girls followed him and sat down on the steps.

"Read it!" commanded Rose. "The showboat's coming!"

Nelly took the sheet of pink paper and began to read aloud. As she read, her eyes widened and a grin of delight spread over her face.

The words were printed in large black letters:

WATCH FOR THE FLOATING PALACE ! ! ! ! !
SEE THE MOST UNUSUAL, THE MOST
STUPENDOUS, MOST GORGEOUS
SHOW ON EARTH ! ! !
SEE THE JAPANESE SWORD SWALLOWER!
THE DANCING GIRLS FROM KASHMIR!
SEE HOKI, THE HINDU ILLUSIONIST, SAW A
LIVING BOY IN HALF!
SEE HIM MAKE A WOMAN DISAPPEAR INTO
SPACE BEFORE YOUR EYES!
SEE THE MOST STIRRING DRAMA IN AMERICA
—*EAST LYNN—LENA RIVERS—UNCLE TOM'S
CABIN—THE MAIL TRAIN*—
BUY YOUR TICKETS EARLY   ADULTS 25 CENTS
CHILDREN 10 CENTS
ARRIVING AUGUST 31   DON'T MISS THE
FLOATING PALACE—ONE OF THE WONDERS
OF THE AGE ! ! !

Written in red ink at the bottom of the page was:
DOCKING AT WILLOW LANDING
IF THE RIVER DON'T RISE.

"The river's not going to rise," said Rose. "We haven't had any rain for a week."

"Well, if it does, they'll go to Sanderson's and that's almost as close," said Nell. "Oh, I can hardly wait!"

"I hope they have the tightrope walker this year," said Callie. She stood up and began to walk an imaginary line, wavering and wobbling as she had seen the tightrope walker do.

"Oh, I can't bear to look at him!" cried Rose, shuddering. She took her handkerchief from the pocket of her skirt and patted her forehead delicately.

"I want to see that boy sawed in half," said Nell.

"And the woman disappear," put in Callie. "Maybe we could find out how he does it and sometime when we wanted to, we could make somebody disappear—Miss Fink, for instance."

"Ugh! Don't mention Miss Fink!" Nell made a sour face.

Miss Fink was the teacher of the small private school which the girls attended. She was not the ogre they would have liked to make their parents think she was. She just believed that duty was duty and that when you came to school, dreams and giggles should be left at home. The children all knew in their hearts that she was right, but it was more fun to pretend that she was cruel and witchlike.

"I wonder where the woman disappears to," said Callie thoughtfully. "And how they get her back."

"Maybe they have to get a new one each time. And a new boy, too. I wonder how they get *them?*"

"They kidnap them," said Callie firmly. "They wait till they come to the show and they pick out two or three and take them away with them."

"Don't be silly," said Rose. "It's just a trick. It's done with mirrors or something."

"I wish it wasn't," Callie declared. "I'd still like to see Miss Fink disappear."

"They'd just get another teacher," Nelly said, looking glum. "I don't see what people have to go to school for, anyway. We could learn all we need to at home."

Aunt Cara appeared in the doorway.

"It's time for lunch," she announced. "You girls come in and wash up. And Nelly, your mother said to take Memphis Belle back to the barn and——"

She was interrupted by a sudden, frightening bellow. It sounded, as Uncle Doctor who had just driven up in his buggy, said, "like a wounded buffalo with a sore throat."

It was, however, only Benjy, who stumbled around the corner of the house bawling and snuffling.

"Whatever in the world is the matter?" cried Aunt Cara, picking up her long skirts and running down the steps. Aunt Rosalie and Nelly's mother appeared in the doorway. Uncle Doctor leaped from his buggy while Missmamma hurried along the hall.

Aunt Cara put her arms around Benjy. "Darling, tell Mamma what happened!" she cried, but Benjy only bawled louder.

"Did you do anything to him?" Nelly's mother asked, looking at her daughter anxiously.

"I pulled his tooth," admitted Nelly, "but that was a long while ago."

"You must have injured him in some way," her

mother said. She went down the steps and leaned over Benjy.

"She hasn't injured him much," said Uncle Doctor, looking at his tear-stained son, "or he couldn't bellow like that. Stop that caterwaulin', Ben, and tell me what's the matter!"

"M—my tooth!" sobbed Benjy. "I—I had it on a string—and th—that old rooster swallowed it!"

"For the love of mud!" cried Uncle Doctor. He pulled out a large handkerchief and held it against Benjy's face. "Blow!" he said while the aunts and Missmamma leaned against each other and laughed and laughed. Uncle Doctor shook his head and walked up the steps. "We eating here?" he asked.

The three families lived so close together that it just seemed natural to eat at whichever house they happened to be in at mealtime. The two men coming home for lunch or supper always said that they drew rein in the road to hear which house had the giggle-gaggle going on in it. For then they knew where the family was gathered.

"Yes," replied Nelly's mother now. "Rena's made gumbo."

"Good!" said the doctor and went into the house.

"Thar She Comes!"

Callie and Rose sat in the big swing on Nell's porch, waiting for her.

"Of course, she's got to stop and feed those horrible cats," said Rose impatiently. "We'll be late."

"Yeah. If she doesn't hurry, we won't even get a good seat, much less see the boat come in," agreed Callie.

A moment later Nell came around the corner of the house. In contrast to Rose, who was neatly dressed in a fresh, starched frock and had on patent leather slippers, Nell looked like a waif. She was barefoot and already hot and dusty. Callie was clean, even though she was barefoot, too. After all, the road would be inches deep in dust and what was more delicious than to feel the hot soft powder under your bare feet?

26

Rose and Callie got up and walked down the steps. When Nell saw them she made an attempt to smooth her unruly curls and shake out the skirts of her dress.

"Old Natchez got stuck up in the barn loft," she explained, wiping her red face with her sleeve. "I had to get up there and get him and he was way over behind some bales of hay."

"Come on," urged Callie. "I thought I heard the whistle just now."

They ran down the short drive from the house to the main road, which was busy with people hurrying down to the levee. A group of Negro children, accompanied by several dogs of every sort of shagginess and leanness, passed just as the girls reached the road. Ahead of them was a straggling crowd of men, women, children, dogs, mules, and a horse and buggy. There was such a cloud of dust that the people seemed to be walking in a fog. Rose took out her handkerchief and held it over her nose and mouth. But Nell took a deep breath. There was a wonderful smell, a mixture of dew on the grass and weeds, the faint odor of the river willows, of dust and dogs and people, and of the river itself moving so lazily through the hot morning sunshine.

The three girls climbed to the top of the levee.

The smell was even better here, for somebody was selling buttered popcorn—some of it was pink!—and people were drinking soda pop and eating great ham sandwiches, just like at a picnic, for they didn't know how long they would have to wait for the *Floating Palace*. The country people had come from miles around to see the showboat dock. They came in broken-down wagons whose wheels spread out as if they had rickets; they came on mules and on horseback, in oxcarts and on foot; and they brought all the children and dogs with them. They sat on the grass and around the dock itself on every bale of cotton, every keg, every pile of lumber or empty box.

Two or three roustabouts were loading a small boat with boxes, and over the sound of the people laughing and talking, the dogs barking and the mules braying, you could hear them singing:

"Captain, Captain, is your money come?
I jest wants to know 'cause I wants to borrow some."

Rose, Callie, and Nell wormed their way through the crowd and down onto the dock. Several people moved aside, speaking to them as they did so. Everybody knew them as "Doctor's children" and "Judge's children," and they were free to go where they pleased.

"Yonder's Bert and Benjy up in the warehouse window," said Nelly, looking at Callie's brothers with envy. "You might know they'd pig the best place."

"They've been down here since daylight, almost," said Callie.

"I hope Benjy doesn't fall out," said Rose anxiously.

"It'd be just like him to, just as the *Floatin' Palace* comes down the river," said Callie heartlessly.

Rose took a small cloth from her pocket and wiped the dust from her patent leather slippers. Then she folded it carefully, dusty side in, and put it back in her pocket.

"Good morning, little ladies," said someone behind them and they turned, recognizing the somewhat metallic tone of their good friend Wang Lee, who ran the grocery store. "Plenty nice day for showboat, huh?" he asked, grinning.

Down along the shore the girls saw their fishermen friends, Pierre and Jean. The men's white teeth flashed in their sun-browned faces as they waved, shouting something the children could not hear in all the noise on the dock.

Suddenly from the distance came the awaited sound—a long drawn-out, mournful whistle.

Dogs barked, a baby cried, even the women yelled excitedly and waved their hats or sunbonnets. The children started dancing jigs, and the roustabouts stopped working and yelled, "Showboat's a-comin'! Thar she comes! Showboat's a-comin'!"

And then came the sound that was the most exciting of all. The black smoke from the little steamboat that powered the *Floating Palace* was joined by a cloud of steam from the calliope. The harsh, wild, ear-splitting music broke upon the summer air so loudly that it drowned out all other sounds.

Right down the middle of the river, between the shanty boats and the fishing boats and the little tugs and the rafts, the big glossy-white showboat with its waving flags, its giant posters advertising all the acts in the show, and its show people standing on the two decks, steamed slowly and steadily, leaving a broad train of foam behind it.

"Oh, I can't wait!" cried Callie, yelling above all the noise. "I can see the captain. I can see the Dancing Girls from Kashmir! Look, Nell, they're all dressed up and standing right out in front!"

"I can see 'em, too, stupid!" said Nell, who felt practically brittle with excitement. She kept jumping from one foot to the other, and even Rose was twisting her handkerchief in her hands and biting her underlip.

You could see the showboat people clearly now. There was Captain Jenkins, his cheeks as red as apples and his white mustaches blowing in the breeze. He wore a blue uniform with brass buttons and waved his blue peaked cap in all directions as the boat steamed ahead.

Perched on his shoulder was a large parrot named Hannibal. Nobody knew how old Hannibal was, but he came with the *Floating Palace* every year. He sat on the boat's railing and called to the people as they came aboard, "Step up and buy your tickets! Don't push, don't shove, please! Plenty for all! Plenty for all!" in his harsh, croaking voice.

Beside the captain stood Mrs. Jenkins, as round and jolly as a jack-o'-lantern, with a big pompadour of pumpkin-colored hair. The two Jenkins sons stood proudly on either side of their parents. And along the railing stood the ladies from Kashmir, their silken robes and pantaloons ballooning in the breeze, their jewels glistening in the sun. Their deep-set black eyes, the lids painted with some strange blue paint, glittered and gazed at all the dazzled people on the levee and the dock. However, the Japanese sword swallower was nowhere to be seen.

"Maybe he has a sore throat," said Nell with a giggle.

But there was a short fat boy, who leaned over the railing of the lower deck and stuck out his tongue at the boys on the levee. "I hope he's the one who gets sawed in two," said Callie.

"They'd never use him to be sawn in two," said Rose, "It would take too long."

All the men who worked on the boat and the people who acted in the plays, the barker who stood on deck and urged the crowd to see the show—even the Negro cook who grinned at everybody from his round, good-natured face—were on deck, waving and nodding and counting the crowd to see if business was going to be good or bad at Willow Landing.

As the *Floating Palace* drew nearer, the sound from the calliope was ear-splitting, the Kashmir dancing girls waved and fluttered wildly, and the boy lost his balance and had to be snatched by the seat of his pants from certain drowning.

"I bet he would float—like a balloon," said Nell disgustedly.

At last the great boat drew alongside the dock. The calliope stopped and for a few moments the silence seemed strange. Then, as the captain stepped closer to the railing and took off his cap again, the crowd cheered loudly. In a moment he waved for quiet and everybody listened, even the hound dogs which had been scratching fleas and a baby who had been bouncing in his buggy.

The captain had a fine deep voice, and he made quite a speech. Everybody had heard it, for he made the same speech every year. But they listened eagerly. It was all about how glad he was to see such a fine crowd out, what a stupendous show they were going to see, and how they must come early and get their tickets, because the show was so popular they might not get seats.

"Don't push, don't shove!" screamed Hannibal. "Plenty for all!"

The captain reached up and put his hand over Hannibal's beak.

He bowed, his wife bowed, his two sons bowed, and the dancers from Kashmir disappeared into the boat with strange, slow wiggles and everybody cheered again. Only the boat's cat, a lean tiger with round yellow eyes, stayed to stare back at the people.

After this the crowd drifted away, although most of the boys stayed, hanging around the showboat to see how much they could see for nothing and in hopes of getting a job that would take them inside.

The girls turned to walk back up the levee. Callie saw her father, Uncle Doctor, sitting in his buggy and watching the crowd. She knew that he enjoyed the showboat as much as anybody and would be right there for the first performance if nobody called him out for a broken arm or a stomach-ache.

Only a hundred or so people would come to the show, since Willow Landing was such a small town; but because Uncle Doctor had once done the captain a big favor, the *Floating Palace* never passed without stopping. Once when there was a yellow fever epidemic, the captain had thought he was dying of it. He had anchored the showboat out in the river and yelled to a shanty boatman to send for the doctor. Uncle Doctor had gone out in a fishing boat in spite of everybody's telling him he would die if he went aboard, and had seen the sick man. It turned out that Captain Jenkins had only had malaria, but he never forgot that Uncle Doctor had risked his life to help him. Every year Captain Jenkins sent ten tickets to Uncle Doctor, who promptly gave them to children who could not buy any of their own. But he and his whole family never missed a show.

Halfway up the levee the girls paused to look back at the showboat. The fat boy had come out on

the lower deck and picked up the striped cat. Nelly
watched him with interest. Perhaps he wasn't such
a nasty boy after all, if he liked cats, she thought.

But a moment later she gave a cry of horror. For
the boy had taken hold of the cat by its tail and was

holding it out over the water. The cat mewed and
spit, clawed the air, and tried to clutch the boy's
arm. Its fur rose and it bared its teeth, looking more
angry than frightened.

"Put her down!" yelled Nell. "You beast! Put
her down!"

"Yeah, put her down, Bill," said one of the crew
members.

"All right," said the boy, grinning. He let go of

the cat's tail, and the creature fell into the water with a loud splash.

The boys on the levee cheered, a little girl began to cry, and a woman called out, "You ought to be ashamed of yourself!" at the boy, who stuck his tongue out at her.

All three girls screamed and Nelly cried, "You nasty, nasty boy. I *hate* you!"

"Oh, oh, you're breakin' my heart!" he jeered.

Nelly started down the levee to rescue the cat, which was now swimming desperately toward the shore. Its ears were back, and its eyes were popping out because of fear and dislike of the water. Its fur all wet and plastered down, it was a pitiful sight.

It was only a short distance to the bank and as the cat crawled up on the shore, Nelly stooped over and picked up a good-sized rock. The horrid boy still leaned over the railing, grinning. Nelly wound up as if she were going to pitch a baseball and let the rock fly. It hit Bill with a satisfying "thunk!" and he staggered back, yelling like a stuck pig. The girls turned and ran up the rest of the levee and did not stop until they were out of sight of the boat.

"Nelly Thompson, I'm ashamed of you!" panted Rose. "Throwing rocks right out there in front of everybody! Suppose you'd put that boy's eye out, or hit him in the head."

"I wish she had," said Callie. "He's a bully and a nasty, horrid boy!"

"You wouldn't want me to stand there and let him torture that cat, would you?" Nelly asked indignantly. She stalked ahead, half proud that she had defended the cat, half worried about having acted like a hoodlum. She hoped that Uncle Doctor had driven off before she threw that rock.

At home, they found Bert sitting on Uncle Doctor's front steps, his face dirty and streaked with sweat and his foot wrapped in a white bandage.

"What's the matter?" asked Nell.

"Stepped on a nail," muttered Bert in a hoarse voice. He gave a sniffle and wiped his nose on his sleeve.

"Was it rusty?" asked Callie eagerly.

"I dunno," mumbled Bert. "But it was big. It hurt!" he added and seemed about to burst into tears. You could see that he was struggling against it. A nine-year-old boy doesn't want to cry, especially in front of girls.

"If it was rusty, you'll have lockjaw," said Callie.

Bert turned pale under his smudges.

"I won't either!" he shouted. "Ma soaked it in turpentine. I had to pull the old plank offa me," he added in a self-pitying tone. "It hurt somethin' awful!"

The girls stood around at the foot of the steps and stared at him.

"If you have lockjaw, you can't get your mouth open," said Nell.

"You can't eat or talk," added Callie.

"But he'd have to eat!" cried Rose in distress. "He'd die if he didn't!"

Bert looked as if he were going to die right there on the hot steps.

"I think they knock out your teeth," said Callie, "or at least some of them, so they can feed you through the hole. Of course, you can't have anything but soup or milk or something like that, because you can't chew."

Bert gave a groan and put his hands to his jaws.

"They aren't locked now!" he bellowed hopefully.

"Oh, it takes two or three days for it to come on," said Callie cheerfully.

Bert stood up. "I think I'll go to bed," he said in a low tone and disappeared into the house, limping pitifully.

"You shouldn't have told him all that," said Rose. "You've scared him to death."

"Well, he *could* have it," said Callie. Then she grinned. "I hope I did scare him—good! You remember last week . . . he took my biggest turtle. He claimed he'd caught it, and Mamma made me give it to him. When I took it back he threw it in the river. I may never see it again. So he had something coming to him. I hope he's so scared he *can't* open his mouth!"

"Why, Callie, you're terrible!" said Rose.

"You've just got to get back at boys," said Callie sternly. "If you don't, they'll get everything you have."

"Yeah," said Nelly, thinking of the boy on the showboat. "Boys are awful. I don't know what God made 'em for."

They were eating at Uncle Doctor's that noon, and when Nelly walked into the house she saw him standing in the parlor talking to her mother. The plump doctor's shoulders shook with laughter as he talked, but her mother did not look at all amused. Just as Nelly got to the doorway her mother put her hands to her face and cried, "Oh, no!" She looked over the doctor's shoulder and glared at Nell.

Nelly knew without being told that Uncle Doctor

had been down by the levee when she pitched the rock at the fat boy.

"Oh, Nelly!" cried her mother, looking distressed. "Can't you ever act like a lady? Must you always be so hoydenish and headstrong?"

"Now, Fanny," said Uncle Doctor. "The boy deserved it. Besides, it was a good shot. Couldn't have done better myself."

Nell's mother rolled her eyes heavenward. How could she make a lady of Nell if all her relatives defended her?

"Go and wash up!" she said severely. "You look like a river rat. I'm thoroughly ashamed of you!"

But Nelly wasn't too upset. If it hadn't been for Uncle Doctor, Mamma might have been more angry and said that she couldn't go to the showboat that night. And even if Mamma had, thought Nelly as she lathered her dirty hands with Pear's Soap, she would still be glad that she had hit that boy right in the middle of his fat stomach. Nelly grinned as she remembered his surprised expression. It had been well worth a scolding, she decided.

Lost Hannibal

It was both sad and exciting to go down to the levee the day after the show. It was sad because the place looked so deserted and forlorn. Stubs of tickets, broken pop bottles, pieces of paper and popcorn that had been trampled into the dust, lay all over everything. It was sad because the boat was gone— it usually left in the night right after the show or very early in the morning—and the children knew it would not be back for another year. But it was exciting because you never knew what you would find besides the trash. Sometimes it was a brooch or a child's hat or even a spangle from one of the costumes. If it was something that belonged to somebody at Willow Landing, it was a game to trace the owner and get a reward. The reward was usually a piece of cake or an apple, but it was the hunt for the owner that was fun. The children played detective and searched for clues, even when they knew to whom the article belonged.

When the girls and Bert and Benjy got down to the levee the morning after the show they were surprised to see the *Floating Palace* still there.

The younger Jenkins son was lolling against the railing of the upper deck and Bert said, "What are you doin' here? Are you gonna give another show?"

"Nope," said young Jenkins. "We've lost Hannibal. He flew off somewhere last night, and we can't find him. We've had him so long, he's sorta like one of the family. Pop says we won't have any luck without him, so he's offered a five-dollar reward to anybody that finds him."

"Five dollars!" Bert looked around at his brother and sister and his two cousins. That would be a dollar apiece if they found Hannibal.

"Where do you think he went?" asked Nelly, who had also figured out that five into five went once.

"Well, where would you go if you were a parrot?" asked Bob Jenkins.

"I'd go where there were some other birds," said Nelly promptly. ". . . into the woods."

"Likely," said young Jenkins. "Why don't you look there? We've looked all over town. We don't know our way around the woods and creeks like you all. You might sure enough find him."

The children, delighted at the idea, looked at each other. They turned and climbed up the levee.

Close to the river was the road, and around it clustered the few stores in Willow Landing. A little further off, but not really far, were the houses, and beyond that were the wide cotton fields and the sharecroppers' log cabins. Behind the children's own houses was a large patch of trees, which followed the river for several miles and was almost as wide. In it there were giant oak, walnut, and sweet gum; and along the river, cypress and willows leaned over the water. It was a thick wood full of all sorts of dangers—like snakes and poison ivy, spiders, and possibly spirit creatures.

There was an old graveyard in the woods near where the children lived. The graves were decorated with paper flowers—usually a deep salmon pink—dishes and toys, vases, or little statuettes. Miss-mamma said she thought this was a nice custom. The people did it because they wanted the cherished things of those who had died to be close to them still. The children sometimes wandered in the graveyard on a bright sunny day, reading the inscriptions on the simple tombstones or looking at the objects on the graves. Sometimes the girls gathered wild flowers and put them on their favorite graves.

It was a pleasant enough place then, but on a cloudy afternoon it was plain "spooky," and no child among them would have been caught near it at night.

They had been told over and over again that there was no truth in superstitions and that if anyone told them that when a screech owl gave its weird, quavering cry, somebody was going to die, or that when a black cat crossed your path, it was certain bad luck, they were just telling folk tales and that they were not to be believed.

"Like when Mamma spills the salt and throws it over her shoulder so she won't have bad luck?" Nelly had once asked.

"Yes," Missmamma had answered. "She would have bad luck or she wouldn't, even if she'd never touched the salt, and you know that as well as I do."

Nelly guessed that this was right, but it was really more fun to believe that if fire burns with a blue flame, it means some sort of devilment is afoot, or that a stick's breaking when there's nothing there to break it, is a sure sign a ha'nt is about.

The children often played at the edge of the woods, but they seldom went far into it. But now they thought of the reward and forgot any secret fears they had. They walked bravely into its deep shade.

Bert went first, then Nelly, Callie, Benjy, and Rose, who kept thinking every minute that she could turn back if she wanted to, or if the underbrush got too thick for her taste. They walked slowly, looking up into the trees, pushing their way through the bushes, stopping at the stone wall of the graveyard and every now and then calling, "Hannibal! Oh, Hannibal! Come on, old Hannibal!"

It was very quiet in the woods. Once a jay bird flew down at them, screeching so sharply that Rose screamed and put her hands over her ears. Once Bert thought they were close to a rattlesnake. There was a loud buzzing, and then a large insect—a cicada, or jarfly—flew up and the buzzing ceased. But most of the time the only sound was of their feet shuffling through the leaves and their bodies pushing against the sassafras bushes or scrubby pines.

Once or twice Nelly looked back. They couldn't see the road or any houses now, nothing but woods

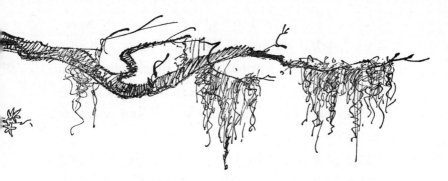

in all directions. She wondered if they had come in a straight line and if they could find their way out. The sky, which had been a sort of muddy blue when they started out, had darkened until the woods were truly fearful-looking. Overhead the trees waved and creaked, their leaves making a sound like rain. And they would have to pass the graveyard going home.

"I don't believe Hannibal would come out here," said Rose. "He's a city bird—at least he's not used to woods."

"But he's a bird," argued Nelly. "He must have come from the forest sometime. Anyway, they've looked everywhere else; Bob Jenkins said so."

"It's going to storm," said Rose. "I'm not going any further."

"You gonna go back by yourself?" asked Bert. Now that the woods were so dark and menacing he didn't think he would want to.

Rose tossed her head. "I'm not afraid of ha'nts,

if that's what you mean. There isn't any such thing anyway, and you know it. I'm much more afraid of lightning, especially out here under the tr——"

Rose had meant to say "trees," but what she ended up saying was "tr——eeeeeeees!"

For just ahead of them they heard a strange, guttural sound, a voice that sounded like no human voice they had ever known.

All the ghosts that they had ever heard of came to the children's minds. There was the headless woman who came looking for her head which an enemy had chopped off. There was the gray man who haunted the river during a fog and was a sure sign of death. There were the vampires who were always looking for healthy people to feed on, and there were the strange creatures—whom almost no one ever saw—who worked voodoo and put conjures on innocent people.

The children stood stock-still, clutching each other. The wood was now full of little noises from the wind and the leaves and the sound of what they hoped were just scurrying creatures. A gopher, hurrying back to some shanty boat along the river bank, ran across Benjy's foot, and Benjy climbed straight up Rose, throwing her to the ground.

As she picked herself out of the brambles and bushes and gave Benjy a hard shake, the sound came again. Huddled together, the children listened fearfully. There seemed to be words, but they could not make them out.

"Let's get outa here," muttered Bert. "I don't think Hannibal would come in here anyway. Like Rose says, he's used to being around people. He's more'n likely in some shanty boat."

He was moving carefully away from the sound of the voice as he talked.

The others started to follow him, but before they had gone two steps, there was a harsh scream, a sound so piteous and appalling that all five of them turned as pale as dust.

Benjy flung his arms around Rose again, and Callie trampled both of them trying to get ahead. More guttural words followed the scream. Horrible pictures of murder and torture, of ghostly creatures, headless or with three eyes, skeletons with gaping eye sockets and wraithlike spirits who melted into the fog, filled the children's minds as they scrambled, getting into each other's way in an effort to leave the place and leave it fast.

Suddenly Nelly, who was in the rear, stopped.

"Wait!" she cried. "Listen! Listen to what it's saying."

Four white faces turned toward her. As they stood there, a heavy wind blew through the wood and there was a quick spatter of rain.

Hannibal Comes Home

The voice came again. The words seemed to have a pattern; they came in short sentences. Somehow they sounded familiar.

"It's Hannibal!" cried Nelly. She turned and ran back toward the sound. The others followed warily.

When they caught up with Nelly she was standing in a sort of clearing under a gigantic dead oak tree. It was stripped bare of leaves and its bark had been ripped by lightning. Evidently the fire set by the lightning had burned a circle of underbrush before the storm had put it out, for there were only stumps and young bushes where Nelly was. The children stood under the tree and looked up.

On a bare limb at the very top sat poor Hannibal. Two jay birds and a thrush were flying about him, pecking at him and pulling out his bright feathers. They lay on the ground like autumn leaves. And poor, naked, worn-out Hannibal was saying over and over in a voice grown hoarse from repeating it, "Don't push, don't shove, please! Plenty for all! Step right up! Don't push, don't shove!"

"For the love of mud!" cried Bert.

"Poor Hannibal! Poor, poor Hannibal!" Rose burst into tears, and Callie wrung her hands.

"Oh, they're killing him!" cried Nelly. "Stop them! Stop them, Bert!"

"How can I stop 'em?" asked Bert reasonably. "I'm way down here, and they're up there."

"Can't you climb up?" asked Rose. "Look, the branches come down real low. Hurry, Bert, climb up and get him!"

"Shoo! Shoo!" Callie screamed, dancing about under the dead tree.

"Get away from there!" yelled Benjy. "Go away, you mean old birds!"

"Those branches are dead," said Bert. "I might get way up there and have one bust with me—then we'd be in a fix. I can't see you girls carrying me home, not with a busted leg or something. Besides, my foot's still sore. I don't think I *could* climb . . ."

"You could try," said Nelly indignantly. "If

you're such a fraidy cat, you won't go up there, I will!"

A second later she had grabbed a lower branch, braced her feet against the tree trunk, and was working her way up.

"Be careful!" cried Rose. "Oh, do be careful! Suppose the limb broke!"

"I'm not gonna climb out on one till I've tried it," Nelly assured her. "They're close together. Even if one broke, I could grab another."

The tree was much taller than it had looked from the ground. Nelly climbed limb after limb. Twice, a branch broke and she had to try another. These were farther apart than the lower ones had been. She began to feel that she might not be able to reach Hannibal after all.

One of the jay birds flew down and flapped in her face screaming, "Thief! Thief! Thief!" Nelly stopped and looked down. Golly, it was a long way down! The other children looked funny, standing there with their faces turned up and their mouths open. Nelly was surprised to find that she was shaking all over.

I hope I don't fall, she thought. Mamma will tell me no lady would ever climb a tree.

She started bravely on again. In another few

seconds she was up to where Hannibal sat. He looked more pitiful than ever from here. His poor bare body was scratched and cold-looking, and his eyes had a frightened look.

Nelly sat in a crotch of the tree and called to him. "Come on, Hannibal! Come to Nelly! Come on, boy!"

Hannibal looked at her wildly as if he thought she was another, bigger enemy.

She held out one hand. "Come on, boy," she said softly. "Come on, Hannibal! Captain wants you, Hannibal. Come on, boy!"

Hannibal had stopped screeching, and the birds had flown off to another tree where they screamed and chattered. The parrot looked at Nelly with his

head first on one side and then the other. He closed
his eyes for a moment and then opened them again
as if he thought Nelly was an apparition and might
vanish if he stopped looking at her. When he saw
that she was still there he shook himself and edged
a step toward her. Nelly held her breath. Hannibal
put his head on one side and eyed her suspiciously.

"Come on, boy, come on!" said Nelly. "Poor
Hannibal."

"Poor bird," agreed Hannibal. "Poor bird!"

"Yes, poor bird," said Nelly. "Come home, Hannibal! Come on, now!"

Hannibal gave a sudden leap and landed on
Nelly's shoulder. It startled her so, that she slipped.
She slid past two branches and heard a horrid
ripping sound. Hannibal gripped her shoulder
with his sharp claws, and she scraped her arm on
the broken bark of the tree. She heard Rose scream
as Bert shouted, "Grab something, Nelly! Hold
on!" and she clutched a branch with both hands
while she hugged the tree with her knees. The
branch held firm and in another minute she had
started down. When she reached the ground she
was shaking badly. She really wanted to cry except that she wouldn't let Bert see her.

"Boy, that was great!" he cried, which made up

for the fright she had had. But when she looked to
see what had ripped she gave a groan, for the whole
back of her dress was torn and hanging like a
train.

"Oh, dear!" she mourned. "What will Mamma
say?"

She looked so unhappy that Rose put an arm
around her. "Don't worry, Nelly," she said. "I'll
mend it when we get home. Aunt Fanny'll never
know. And you were real brave to get Hannibal.
Poor old thing; he looks miserable."

Bert had lifted him from Nelly's shoulder and
was holding him close to his shirt front, because
Hannibal really did look chilly without most of
his feathers.

"I wonder if they'll grow back," said Callie and
began to laugh. "I'm sorry for him," she said between snickers, "but he does look silly. He looks
like old Mr. Postgate."

Nelly grinned in sympathy. Old Mr. Postgate
lived down by the river in a shanty boat that had
been dragged up on the levee. He was quite bald,
with a hooked nose and bright black eyes. He always sat in a chair propped against the house and
smoked while his daughter, who looked almost
as old as he did, did the work.

Hannibal shivered and clutched Bert's finger with his beak as if to remind him that he should be taken home.

"I bet he's hungry," said Nelly. "I bet he's been up there all this time, too scared to come down or to fly off."

"Here," said Benjy, who could always be counted on to have something to eat. He drew a slightly smashed, buttered biscuit from his back pocket and handed it to Hannibal.

The parrot reached out and clutched it with one claw. Then he looked about at them as if puzzled as to what to do with it. He turned his half-bald head sideways and stared at the biscuit.

"Polly want a cracker!" wheezed Hannibal in his new hoarseness that was almost like a sizzle.

"Well, I haven't got a cracker," said Benjy. "Eat what's put before you," he added, remembering what Missmamma always said to him.

"Yeah, don't be so choosy," said Nelly, whose scraped arm was stinging badly. "You're lucky we had a biscuit with us."

"Put him on your shoulder, Bert," said Rose. "I think he's used to standing on his perch when he eats."

Bert lifted the bird slowly and set him on his own

shoulder, flinching as the gray claws dug into him. Hannibal, standing on one foot, wobbled a little and then lifted the biscuit to his curved beak. He took a large bite and swallowed it. Then he croaked, "Plenty for all! Plenty for all!" and took another bite.

It was almost as dark as night in the woods now. The trees bent and creaked in the strong wind. Worse than that, there were several flashes of lightning followed by such close claps of ear-splitting thunder that the children knew the storm was right upon them.

"We ought to get out from under all these trees," said Rose as they pushed their way through the wet underbrush. "It's the worst place we could be in, in a storm."

They remembered the stark tree in which they had found Hannibal and the ground around it, all laid bare by lightning. Suddenly the woods were frightening. They hurried on.

They were so intent upon their own fears and so hampered by the brambles and scrubby underbrush that they did not see the horrid boy from the boat until they ran into him. He was standing there in the deep wood facing them. His hair was plastered down on his forehead giving him an even stupider look, and he had a thoroughly nasty expression in his small green eyes.

"Gimme that bird!" he said roughly. "Hand him over! I found him. I found him a while ago. I was just lookin' for a long stick to knock him down with."

"I bet you *would've* knocked him down!" cried Nelly indignantly. "And you weren't even where he was. You were just coming this way. You hadn't been anywhere near that—that place where we found him!"

"Yeah. Where did we find him?" asked Bert, whose sore foot was hurting him and who was not only cold but was being pinched by Hannibal's claws. "Tell me that! Where did we find him?"

"How do I know?" asked Bill. "He coulda moved since I saw him, but I saw him first."

"Where did you see him?" asked Rose.

"He was settin' up in a tree," said the boy smartly.

"How could you see him for the leaves?" asked Rose.

"Oh, I could see him all right, all red-and-yeller feathers. You wait till I tell Captain Jenkins you pulled all the feathers off him. I bet you won't get to see no shows after that! Now give him here!"

He reached for the shivering parrot, who had

evidently had enough punishment for one day. As Bill thrust his hand out toward Hannibal, the old bird leaned forward and gave the boy's fingers a nasty nip. At the same time a blinding flash of lightning struck a tree somewhere in the woods and Callie screamed like a panther.

It was too much for Master Fatty. He yelped like a scalded hound dog and turned to run. It was amazing to the children how fast he could get through the underbrush. They decided afterward that he mashed down the bushes by the sheer weight of his body. Anyway he made a broad path for them, and they followed close on his heels. When they got to open ground Bill kept going, holding his hands—Bert noticed with satisfaction that one was bleeding—over his head as if he thought he could ward off the storm.

Poor Hannibal drooped against Bert's cheek, as if he had used his last strength against the boy. Bert shifted the parrot to the inside of his shirt, which was soaking wet but might keep the wind off it.

"Gosh, I hope he doesn't die," he said gloomily.

"At least not before we get him home," said Callie. "They didn't say, 'dead or alive.'"

"Poor Hannibal!" said Rose. "You shouldn't be

thinking of money now, Callie. Think of poor Hannibal."

"I'm thinking of poor Callie," said Callie crossly. "I'm wet to the skin and I'll have a sore throat for sure." As if to prove that she might become ill she sneezed so loudly that Hannibal woke up and croaked in a hoarse whisper:

"Don't push! Don't shove!"

There was nobody on the road, and only one or two faces appeared at the cabin windows as they trudged along toward the levee. They hurried down the bank and across the landing plank. The big boat rocked gently on the water. Rain was falling hard now and it made lots of small plopping sounds in the river.

The Jenkinses lived in the little steamboat that pushed the great showboat up and down the river. The children had glimpsed the living quarters before, and now they walked to the door of the stateroom, which the Jenkinses used for a parlor, and knocked. In a moment Mrs. Jenkins opened it, looking out curiously.

"Well, forevermore!" she cried when she saw them. "If it isn't the Doctor's children!" Then she saw Hannibal. "They've got Hannibal!" she called over her shoulder, and then turned back to the children. "But what ever have you done to him?"

"Nothing," said Bert sulkily. After all they'd been through to get this old bird, it was too much to be accused again of having done something to him. "We found him way out in the woods."

"In a tree," said Rose. "And the birds—"

"Were picking his feathers off," said Nelly, "and he——"

"He was hollerin! 'One at a time! Don't push, don't shove! Plenty for all!'" screamed Callie, giggling and shivering.

Even Mrs. Jenkins had to laugh, and the captain, who had come to see what the racket was about, leaned against the side of the boat and laughed like a jolly Santa Claus.

"He's cold," said Nelly at last. "And I think he's worn out."

"Poor old bird," said Mrs. Jenkins, wiping her eyes with her apron. "I bet he is at that." She took the parrot from Bert's shoulder and held him close. "Why, he's shivering all over," she said. "I'll get something and wrap him in it," she added, bustling into the boat.

"You all come on in," said Captain Jenkins. "You're soaking wet. Ma, get something for these children to drink—something hot—they're wet to the skin!"

Once inside, the children stood and stared. The parlor was a small room as all steamboat cabins are, and it was so crowded that at first they did not see how they could all fit in. There was a fireplace with a large fan-shaped piece of paper painted to look like flames in front of it. On the mantel were all sorts of objects that fascinated them: a china pig with a rose in its mouth, a vase filled with what looked like hollyhocks, some fishing tackle, a large round stone, two little china figures representing David Copperfield and Oliver Twist, a number of papers and books; and right in the center there was a sort of statue of a group of people sitting around an old stove whittling, reading the newspaper and so on while a small child played on the floor with a large furry cat. The statue was all made of brownish clay, and Nelly and Callie stared at it in amazement.

The walls were hung with dozens of pictures of the *Floating Palace*, of the Jenkins family and the various members of the crew and the cast, and with scenes from several plays. Besides all this there were fat little stuffed chairs, a round table with a green felt cloth, shelves filled with fancy cups and saucers with the names of cities on them, and numerous other objects that the children could not take in all at once. In one corner on a tiny kerosene stove a kettle bubbled cheerfully.

Mrs. Jenkins came hurrying back. She had wrapped Hannibal in one of the baby blankets used in the plays. Only his head stuck out, and he looked more like Mr. Postgate than ever. She put him in a basket and then said, "I had just put the kettle on. Why don't you have a cuppa with us?"

"You see, my old lady came from England," said Captain Jenkins, "so long ago you might never know it to hear her talk now. But she still remembers that her folks always had what they calls their 'elevenses,' which means a snack about the middle of the morning."

"I would like some elevenses," said Nelly, shivering.

"And you shall have some, love," said Mrs. Jenkins.

"Sit you down," said the captain. He pushed forward a little stuffed chair, a footstool, and a sort of loveseat on which Benjy, Callie, and Nelly managed to squeeze. His own captain's chair was brown with worn arms, and for herself Mrs. Jenkins obviously used the old rocker near the stove.

Now she bustled about and brought out a large loaf of homemade bread and seven cups and saucers. "The cast has their own elevenses in their rooms if they like," she said. "Papa and I like to be alone sometimes, present company excepted," she added, wagging her head and laughing. Her large red pompadour fell over one eye, and she pushed it back with a surprisingly white hand on which shone a ring with an enormous green stone.

"I must give you the reward for finding Hannibal," said the captain as the kettle began to boil. He took out his black leather purse, which had a brass snap on it, and from a fat roll of bills drew a five-dollar one.

Bert looked at Rose, and she knew that he wanted to say, "Shall we tell him?"

She hated to, because it seemed a shame that anybody as mean as that boy should get any credit, much less the money. But she had to be honest, so she cleared her throat and said, "Maybe we didn't find him first. That boy from the showboat—he met us in the woods and said he'd seen Hannibal first."

"But he was just gettin' there!" said Bert angrily. "He hadn't even gotten to the tree where we found Hannibal!"

The captain and his wife looked at each other, and Mrs. Jenkins frowned and nodded.

"It's just as I told you," she said. "That Bill is a young rascal. It seems strange to me that both times Hannibal has disappeared he has 'found' him and claimed the reward."

"You may be right," said the captain. "Anyway, Doc's children have brought the old bird home, and I'd take their word against Bill's any time."

"He said he was looking for a stick," said Callie. "He was goin' to knock Hannibal out of the tree!"

"I'd just like to catch him at it," said Mrs. Jenkins, her eyes flashing. "I'll take care of that young man when I see him."

Then Captain Jenkins held out the five-dollar bill.

"Who gets it?" he asked, holding it up.

"We all do," said Rose, "but give it to Bert to carry."

Mrs. Jenkins brought an enormous teapot from where it had been warming at the back of the little stove. She put in the tea and poured the boiling water from the kettle. Next she placed a large tea cozy over the pot. Then she began cutting thick slices of bread and spreading them with creamy butter.

"What about the raspberry jam?" said the captain. Mrs. Jenkins reached up on a shelf and brought down a fat brown jar.

She picked up the tea cozy and set it gently on the mantel.

"Now draw up," said the captain, pulling his own chair toward the table. "I've found that 'elevenses' isn't a bad custom even if it does come from the old country."

The tea was almost black by now, but when they had put lots of sugar and good rich cream in it, it tasted wonderful. And it was so blessedly hot! The children drank several cups apiece with slices of the good brown-crusted bread and raspberry jam.

As the tea warmed them they began to chatter. They told the captain and his wife how they had found Hannibal, how scared they had been, and how terrible it had been to see the birds pulling off Hannibal's feathers. When they told how Hannibal had just sat there saying, "Don't push, don't shove!" the captain laughed and laughed all over again.

"That's a good one!" he cried. "That's a good one!" He handed Hannibal a bit of crust.

When she could eat no more, Nelly leaned back and rubbed her stomach, ignoring Rose's frown at her. "When I'm grown up and have a house of my own," she said, "I'm always going to have 'elevenses.'"

Mrs. Jenkins laughed, a large soft laugh that made her shake all over.

"We really must go," said Rose, getting out of her chair where she left a damp spot because she really was "soaked to the skin."

"I'm glad we found Hannibal. I hope he gets his feathers back, and thank you so much for the tea."

"Yes, it was scrumptious," said Callie, running her tongue around her mouth to get off the last luscious bit of jam and butter.

The others got up—all leaving damp spots—and backed out of the room, Nelly clutching her torn skirt behind her, thanking the captain and his wife.

"And thank you for Hannibal," said Mrs. Jenkins. "If he never grows any feathers, I'll knit him a sweater!"

Natchez in Disgrace

Rose forgot to mend the dress Nelly had torn while looking for Hannibal, and Aunt Fanny had plenty to say, just as Nelly had feared she would.

Nelly was made to stay at home for two whole days and to wash the cats she had forgotten to wash before the showboat's arrival.

It was a wet, messy job and the cats howled in protest, running about the yard, shaking their legs and themselves, and splattering water all over Nelly and Rena, who was helping her. They looked so skinny and miserable with their hair plastered down and their eyes fairly popping out with fright and indignation, that not even their antics at trying to dry themselves could make Nelly laugh.

The hot summer sun soon dried them, however.

A satisfactory number of dead fleas and the softness of the cats' fur, which she brushed with a dolls' hairbrush when it was dry, made Nelly feel that it had been a good morning's work after all.

On the third day after Hannibal's return, the aunts went to Natchez to purchase winter clothes for all the children. They went on the steamer *J. M. White,* and the children went down to the landing to see them off. They stood staring after the boat as it moved slowly down the wide muddy river.

"I wish we were going too," said Callie.

"Not me," said Nelly, and Rose laughed.

The children's other grandmother lived at Natchez, and Nelly was a constant disappointment to her. She was a dignified old lady of French descent who put a great deal of stress on young ladies being young ladies and knowing all the social arts and graces. She was married to a rough-and-ready Irishman from whom "Nelly surely got her wild ways," her grandmother often remarked.

Nelly adored her grandfather and she liked to visit in Natchez, but she did not like being made to mind her p's and q's and being constantly chided by her grandmother about her tomboy ways. Besides, when their mothers were away the children felt as if they were having a sort of holiday of their

own. Missmamma openly spoiled them; and Uncle
Doctor, who was always fun, paid them more atten-
tion. Even Uncle Judge, who was usually busy and
seemed to live in a world of his own, unbent enough
to read to them or take them on rides about the
country.

It was still early in the morning when they
turned and walked back up to the levee, and they
wondered what to do. This was Missmamma's day
to play cards with her friends, and the uncles, of
course, were out about their businesses. The children
ambled along the road, which was still damp after
the rain a day or so before. The mud lay in soft
swirls and ridges that were fun to mash down with
their bare feet. Benjy and Bert went off on some
business of their own, and the girls walked back to
their houses.

At home they wandered around the yard. The
last "old maids" and nasturtiums in Missmamma's
garden were in full bloom, and the shiny fat buds of
the chrysanthemums showed little slivers of yellow
or white or red through the golden green.

From Rose's yard they moved through Callie's
and then on to Nell's, sucking the tip of a nastur-
tium flower for its spicy honey, catching a grasshop-

per to make him "spit tobacco," stirring a doodlebug hole to make him "come up and get his bread." All these were just ways of passing the time on a hot summer morning.

At Nelly's they found Rena sitting on the back steps of her cabin with her apron over her head, rocking back and forth and wailing in heartbroken tones.

"Why, Rena!" cried Nelly, running up and putting her arms around her. "What in the world? What's happened?"

Rena continued to wail until Nelly pulled the damp apron aside and said, "Come on, now! Bawling isn't going to help anything. What's the matter?"

Poor Rena's eyes were swollen almost shut. Her lips quivered as she said angrily, "That old Natchez cat—he done killed my frizzly chicken!"

"Oh, no!" cried Nelly, shocked. "How do you know it was Natchez? Did you see him?"

"It was Natchez, all right," said Rena in a hoarse voice. "He come around the house, draggin' that po' little spindly thing. He'd done et the head off!"

"Ooooh!" cried Rose, putting her hands over her ears as if she couldn't bear to hear more.

"Was it dead?" asked Callie.

"Of course, stupid!" cried Nelly, who was not only shocked, but whose heart bled for Rena and her cruelly slaughtered chicken. "Try gettin' your head chewed off, and you'll see whether you're dead or not! Oh, Rena, I'm so sorry! Poor little thing! Can we bury it for you? I'm going to whip that Natchez till his eyes bug out!"

Rena sniffled and wiped her eyes with the apron. "There ain't nothing left to bury," she said so mournfully that Nelly's eyes filled with tears, and Rose came over and gave Rena a squeeze around the shoulders. "I run after that ol' devil, and he took off to the woods. My po' little chicken's gone now!" and she began to sob afresh.

The children knew that this strange little chicken, whose feathers curled up at the ends and gave it a "frizzly" appearance, was Rena's particular pet. It followed her about the yard and even into her house, and in the wintertime she had a box by the open fire where it sat and watched the flames as contentedly as a dog or cat.

"I'll just have to get you another one," said Nelly at last. But she felt simply awful. Another one would not be Rena's special pet, her own little frizzly; nor would it make up for the cruel thing

that old Natchez had done. Nelly thought woefully
that there really were some cats who did not deserve to be loved.

She thought of the round silver dollar in her
bureau drawer—her part of the reward for finding
Hannibal. None of the girls had spent their money.
It was such fun to think of all the things it could
buy, more fun than spending it on just the one or
two things that they would actually get for it. She
sighed, wondering what a frizzly chicken would
cost, and if her dollar would buy one.

The girls looked at each other. They knew that
there was but one thing to do. "Don't cry any
more," said Nelly, getting up and patting Rena on

the back. "We'll get you another one—I'll get you one if I have to *make* it!"

This struck Callie as ridiculous and she gave a nervous giggle.

"And when Natchez comes back," said Rose to Rena, "you catch him and give him a switching he won't forget. If he's going to kill chickens, Nelly just can't keep him."

By this time, Nelly looked almost as gloomy as Rena. But she went into the house and got her dollar from the little box in which she kept her pins and beads. The others joined her silently and they walked out of the yard to begin their search for a frizzly chicken.

"I wonder where we ought to go?" asked Rose. "The only people I know with frizzly chickens are all like Rena; they wouldn't sell 'em for diamonds."

"Let's go to Wang Lee's," said Nelly. "Sometimes he buys a lot of chickens at one time, so he might just happen to buy a frizzly."

"Well, it would be 'just happen,'" declared Callie. "You couldn't even make one chicken croquette from a frizzly."

"Yeah," agreed Nelly. "I don't reckon Wang Lee would be dumb enough to buy one. But I think I'm going there anyway. He might know somebody who had one, and besides, if I go around with this dollar in my hand, whoever's got a chicken to sell will think I mean to pay a dollar for it and they'll charge me that much."

"Maybe a frizzly will cost that much," said Rose, "since people think so much of 'em."

"But if they don't, I sure don't want to spend my whole dollar on one," argued Nelly. "So I'm going to get some change from Wang Lee."

The Chinese grocer's store was at the other end of Willow Landing's only street, but it was just a five-minute walk. The girls hurried along the warm, still damp road past the little stone post-office building, past the vacant lots beyond it, past the furniture-and-undertakers, past Mr. Edmonds' drugstore, which was a front room in his house where he mixed up prescriptions and played chess with Uncle Doctor. There were two or three empty store buildings which somebody had built when they thought Willow Landing was going to be a big town, and then finally Wang Lee's grocery store.

It was more than a grocery store, because it carried bright tin buckets, pieces of harness, sometimes a saddle or two, lots of rope and wire ties for tying cotton bales, dress materials—mostly cheap calico for cotton-pickers' dresses—and sunbonnets, glass

lamps and lanterns, work gloves and tools. There were shelves of canned goods and on the counter was a large glass case filled with doughnuts and pies made by Mrs. Woodly over at Greenville. She drove over twice a week, bearing her delicious and fragrant cargo.

There was always an open barrel of pickles in the store—the great juicy things floating like waiting sea monsters beneath the briny scum on top of the liquid. The cracker barrel stood open, too, and almost everybody who came in reached for a free "sody" cracker. The top ones were sometimes dusty, because Wang Lee had just shooed his big Persian cat, Sunflower, out of the barrel where she loved to sleep.

There was a wonderful stout smell of coffee, cheese, pickles, spices, tar and rubber, tobacco, which hung in great dark twists against the wall, leather and kerosene (called "coal oil"), naphtha soap, and salted fish and smoked ham.

Wang Lee was weighing up coffee when the cousins went into the store. He looked up and smiled at them. "Good morning, little missies. You want something?"

"Do you all happen to have a frizzly chicken?" asked Nelly.

Uncle Judge had explained to the children when they were quite small that there is no letter R in the Chinese language, and that words like "rice" and "try" and "rat" were hard for Chinese people to pronounce. So the children were not surprised when Wang Lee said, "We got white chickens, dominecker chickens, Lode Island Led Chickens, old Leghorn looster—but no flizzly chicken. What you want with flizzly chicken, no how?"

They told him about what had happened to Rena's little frizzly and how badly she wanted another one.

"I'll pay for it if I can find one," said Nelly.

Wang shook his head. "Too bad. Velly solly, we have no flizzly chicken. But if I see one, I tell you quick, huh?"

"Thank you," said Nelly, "and oh, Wang, I wish you would change this dollar for me. I'll take a dime's worth of lemon drops," she added because she felt that if Wang did her a favor, she should buy something from him.

"Surely, surely!" cried Wang. He picked up a little striped paper bag and turned to the glass case where the candy was displayed—peppermints, lemon drops, licorice sticks, and fat chocolate drops. With his little tin scoop he shoveled up the candy and filled the sack. Then he opened a tin box and took out the change for the dollar.

Thanking him again, Nelly put the change in the deep pocket that the aunts and Missmamma always made in the girls' skirts, and grasping the little paper sack, she led the way out of the store.

Search for a Frizzly

"Let's try the shanty boats," said Rose. "They always have chickens, and they're mostly glad to sell anything."

Without a word, the girls turned toward the part of the river bank where the willows grew so thick you could not see through them, and walked along the levee.

When they reached the willow groves they climbed down the levee on a narrow, crooked path and stopped in front of the first of a cluster of small houseboats. Some of these were tied to stakes on the bank and rocked gently in the water. Some had been pulled up onto the land and sat on big chunks of log or stones. All of them were shabby and dirty and full of fascinating people and things.

In the first one, which was floating on the river, a large red-faced woman stood washing at a big tin tub. She was barefoot and her skirts were tucked up, held by a rope around her waist which kept them out of her way. She wore a large straw hat with a hole in the top from which her black hair spurted like a fountain. On the deck beside her a fat baby, tied with a rope to the boat's railing, sat chewing a piece of bacon rind while a scrawny hound dog lay and watched it with hungry eyes. Mosquitos buzzed about, and as the woman splashed and sloshed the clothes in the water, she talked to somebody in the house.

"An' Ben said he seen a' alligator long's this boat, right off that sandbar beyond Barker's landin'."

From inside the house there was a rumble and the woman said, "I don't know if he was lyin' or not— but that's what he said. Lawsee, if here ain't Doc's chillun! Howdy, you all."

She stood up and wiped her face with a soapy red arm and beamed.

"Mornin', Miz Benson," they said in a chorus, and Nelly added:

"Howdy, Lily Pearl." The baby smiled and patted her hands together.

"Don't untie her," said Mrs. Benson, bending

over her tub again. "Mr. B's got the misery in his
joints this mornin', and if she fell in, I don't know
who'd get her out."

The children sat down on the deck or draped
themselves over the railing and admired Lily Pearl.
She was a pretty child once you looked under the
grease and dirt. Her eyes were large and blue, and
her hair was a mass of tangled yellow curls.

They didn't stay long at the Benson boat. They
knew the Bensons had no chickens. They had only
stopped because it would have been rude not to
speak to them.

Presently, they walked on to where an even more
dilapidated shanty was pulled up on the shore.
Hound dogs lay around in the dust, and a scattering
of chickens walked among them, scratching at the
soil. As the cousins came into sight two children
peered out of the house and then with a yell rushed
out to meet them.

"Where you all goin'?" asked a boy of about ten.
He had a shock of black hair and bright, laughing
brown eyes. A little girl of nine with sandy hair and
blue eyes stood by, grinning.

"Just around," said Rose.

And Nelly added, "You know anybody who's
got a frizzly chicken for sale?"

"No, I don't," said the boy, whose name was
Lester. "An' Ma and Pa's gone shrimpin'. Grandpaw's here. Come on in and see him."

The children trooped into the shanty. It was
dim and hot inside. There were only two rooms in
the place and in this one the family did their cook-
ing and most of their living. Behind it was a smaller
room where some of them slept. Grandpaw was
sitting in a rocking chair by the hearth, smoking
a pipe.

This room was fairly tidy in spite of being
crowded. Shanty people were always poor. They
didn't have much furniture, but they didn't seem
to need it. A stove or fireplace to cook on, a table to
eat on, a few boxes for chairs, and pallets on the
floor which could be stuffed out of the way in the
daytime, seemed to suit them fine.

They did have a lot of strange things, though,
and Bert and Benjy and the girls were always in-
terested in these. There was a hornet's nest and a
large turtle shell hanging on the wall along with
a faded calendar several years old with the picture
of a beautiful girl sitting under a weeping willow.
It was dated 1895 and most of the leaves of the
calendar part were gone. Here and there a nail
had been driven in the wall and the family's

clothes hung on these. In these little houses there
were always odd bits of driftwood, cheap ornaments,
and a surprising assortment of things that the shanty
people picked up after floods—a broken dish which
was plenty good enough to hold "somethin' that
didn't run," the foot of a once-pretty bed, a chipped
wash basin, a doll baby, or a piece of iron fencing.
Everywhere you looked in a shanty house there was
something you would never see at home.

A long chain was looped over one arm of Grandpaw's rocking chair, and the other end of it was
attached to the collar of a fat raccoon sitting on its
haunches, eating a piece of biscuit.

"Howdy," said Grandpaw as the children came
in, "me an' Coony-boy is jest havin' a bite t' eat." He
took a loud sip of coffee from the saucer he held
in his gnarled, sunburned hand. The coon stopped
nibbling and stared at the children suspiciously.
Then it dipped the biscuit into a small pan of water
on the hearth and began chewing on it again.

The children were delighted to see the raccoon.
Grandpaw had had it as far back as they could remember, and he was always full of tales about the
tricks Coony had been up to. They sat on the floor
around it now and watched it eat.

"I got him tied up," said Grandpaw. "It's got

so, I can't trust him in the house no more at all. He took Maw's snuff and poured it all out the winder —on the river side of the shanty, too. It's floated clear down to Natchez by now. Maw's fit to be tied without her snuff," he added. "Lallie Bell's done gone over to the store to git her some more. She said I oughta switch Coony for doin' it, but, law, he don't know no better."

He looked at the little creature lovingly and Coony, as if he knew Grandpaw was his best friend, cocked his head sideways and grinned up at him. The children laughed and Nelly said, "He got such cute little black paws. Oh, look! He's handing me a piece of his biscuit." The little coon was, indeed. He had broken off a damp piece of dough and held it out to her.

"Won't be long now," said Grandpaw, wiping his chin on his sleeve, "till the pecans come in. Coony do love pecans. He's a big help, too, crackin' 'em."

The children had seen them many times, sitting by the fire and cracking the nuts which the rest of the family gathered. Coony ate about every other one he cracked with his sharp little teeth, but he handed enough of the nuts he cracked to Grandpaw to make him seem like a real helper. The old man picked out the sweet, rich meats and put them in paper sacks. Some of these they sold, but most of them they kept to eat during the winter. Lallie Bell, Grandpaw's youngest, made fudge and molasses candy with pecans in it, and in the children's minds nothing was better.

"A frizzly chicken?" repeated Grandpaw, when they asked him about one. "Seems like I seen one a while back, but I don't recollect where."

He thought for a moment, peering under his glasses to where the willows leaned in at the window. "Now ... let ... me see," he said slowly. "Oh, yes! Yessiree. I seen a frizzly right here on the river. Feller had it on a boat—on the way t' New Orleans, he was. 'Bout a week ago. Said it was his little gal's pet. Yeah, I seen a frizzly chicken. Why?"

Disappointed, the children explained that they wanted to buy one, not just hear about it. Grandpaw shook his head. "This un's about down to Biloxi by now," he said.

They played a while with the shanty-boat children, looking at an extra-large crawfish which the boy, Lester, had in a tin can, and then they wandered on.

The path along the river's edge was damp and covered with old willow leaves, weeds, and bits of trash washed up by the river. It had a boggy smell that the children liked. Occasionally a sulky-looking turtle would waddle out of the way as they passed, and swim lazily out into the water or draw in his head and legs and try to look like a stone. A heron flew up and stretched long, awkward wings, sailing across to the other side as they stopped to watch him.

The next shanty was closed—locked tight—and apparently empty. Only the shaggy-looking dog lying on the shore beside it, showed that the boat was lived in. A big sign on a tree near-by said:

FRESH FISH - SHRIMP

And another one tacked on a second tree read:

NO SHOUTIN
NO HOLLERIN

The smell of the river bank was stronger here, because all around the shanty boat were the pink shells and tails of shrimp. On the landing plank that went from the shore to the boat a jay bird sat and pecked at a fish head. It flew up screeching as the children came near the boat.

They were disappointed to find the shanty boat closed. This was where Pierre and Jean, their two shrimp-boat friends, lived. The men were brothers and had come from further down the river because of something that had happened in New Orleans. The children didn't know what it was, but they liked to think that it was something very mysterious, perhaps even a murder.

Nobody seemed less like murderers than Pierre and Jean La Rue, however. They were friendly and cheerful and always willing to stop and talk to the children. They often took them out on the river in their little fishing boat and that was something to remember!

The wind made ripples in the water, and the river looked miles wide when you were out in the middle of it. The big nets, trailing along through the water, would come up full of small wriggling brown shrimp when Pierre and Jean hauled them in. Later they would all go back to the shanty boat together. Jean would cut off the shrimp heads neatly and quickly with a ferocious-looking knife; Pierre would put a kettle on the stove, throw in some salt, garlic, and bay leaf, and in no time the shrimp would come out pink and delicious. Then they would all sit on the deck and eat them, shelling the shrimp like peanuts and throwing the pale pink shells into the water.

It was not everybody, the children often thought, who had friends like Pierre and Jean, and they were disappointed not to find them at home this morning.

"Let's go see Charlie Wildhorse," said Nelly.

Charlie Wildhorse was a Choctaw Indian who also lived in a shanty boat and made willow baskets for a living. The girls didn't care much about going to see him, because he never had much to say. Sometimes he brought them tiny baskets no bigger than a walnut, and once when Callie had chicken pox he had made her a little cage and put a chipmunk in it. But the chipmunk gnawed his way out after having bitten Benjy, and Callie was not really sorry, since she could not bear to see wild things shut up. She was not sorry—much—about Benjy's finger either, because she had asked him to stop poking it into the cage.

"I don't want to go see Charlie," said Rose. "He's always chewing tobacco, and his shanty's so dirty."

"It's not, either!" said Nelly, who admired Charlie tremendously. "He just has to have all that stuff to work with. It's not his fault he hasn't got a bigger house."

"It's his fault he never washes his skillet," said Rose, wrinkling her nose, "nor his face, either, as far as I can tell."

"That's it; you can't tell," muttered Nelly. "You oughta be ashamed, talkin' about him when he's all the time giving you things."

"Well, I wouldn't do anything to hurt him," said Rose in a superior way, "but I don't have to like being around him."

"Anyway," said Callie, "he hasn't got any chickens, and you know how he is, he always says he doesn't know anything about his neighbors. He probably wouldn't tell you if he knew somebody who had a frizzly-chicken *farm!*"

"I know!" said Rose, who felt that since she wouldn't go to Indian Charlie's, she ought to have a helpful idea. "You know those shacks way down on Crawdad Row? All those people have chickens. They've got domineckers and game chickens and ducks and turkeys, and I bet they have some frizzly chickens."

Nelly hesitated. Crawdad Row ran through a heavily wooded section along the river bank. The gigantic water oaks were hung with shrouds of thick gray moss. It was almost dark under the trees, and the whole place had a spooky, mysterious air.

Except for the clucking and crowing of the chickens or the barking of one of the many hound dogs,
there never seemed to be any sound in all of the
dim woods. And the people who lived there were
strange and secretive. They were part Spanish, part
Indian or French, and they had queer ways of doing
things. Nobody had ever forbidden the children to
go there, but they knew as well as if they had been
told, that it was not a place their parents would have
wanted them to go.

They stood on the path among the willows and
stared at each other. Each knew what the others
were thinking and finally Nell said, "Well, we've
just got to find Rena a frizzly!"

So Rose shrugged and turned toward the higher
road which led into the woods, and the two younger
girls followed her.

Frizzly Come, Frizzly Go

For about a quarter of a mile, the road lay between the cotton fields of a big plantation on which not one inch of space was given to trees or shade. The early afternoon sun was hot; the damp earth beneath their feet was rapidly turning to dust. Under the sunbonnets their faces got pinker and pinker with the heat, and they walked more and more slowly. At last they saw the thick group of trees and just within it two small log houses.

"I feel like Columbus when he first saw land," said Nelly, taking off her sunbonnet and wiping her hot face. "I sure hope we find a frizzly at one of these cabins!"

They knocked at the first two houses, but no one answered. The doors and windows were shut and

95

there was a deep silence about. Here under the thick trees it seemed lonesome and a little scary.

At the third house a large, bony woman came to the door and glared at them as if she thought they meant to do her some harm.

At first she said she did not have any frizzlies, but when Nelly reached into her pocket and brought out a handful of change, the old woman stood there for a long moment without saying anything, as though she were trying to make up her mind to part with her treasure.

"How much you give?" she asked at last.

"Twenty-five cents?" said Nelly hopefully. She had wanted to buy a paint box with the money Captain Jenkins had given her.

The old woman laughed a long, slow, nasty laugh showing her almost toothless gums. Nelly looked at Callie in despair and Callie, suddenly angry, said, "Well, how much do you want for one? You ought to be glad to sell one; they're not worth anything anyhow."

"Then why you want one?" asked the old woman sharply.

"We don't," said Nelly. "But we have a friend . . . we love her very much and . . . and . . . my cat ate her pet frizzly. I'm just trying to get her another one because I feel so sorry for her. Please sell us one! I'll pay you all I can." She sat down on the steps and spread out the dimes and nickels.

The old woman's eyes brightened at the sight of the money. Her lips moved as if she were counting it and she said suddenly, "I sell one she-frizzly for one dollar."

Nelly's heart sank. She had only ninety cents.

"I've only got ninety cents," she said anxiously. "Please, won't that do? Maybe I could bring the other ten cents tomorrow or the day after."

The woman said nothing. She must be part Indian, thought Nelly. She was so sparing with words, and her face had the same shape as some of the Choctaws she had seen. Nelly was deathly afraid of all Indians except Charlie Wildhorse. Suddenly this little settlement seemed very far from home. She looked about and saw that no one seemed to be in any of the other houses. Then there was a movement in one of the windows, and she knew they were being watched.

Callie, too, began to feel that they were very alone out here. She moved closer to Nelly, who swallowed and said bravely, "Will you sell her for ninety cents?"

The old woman frowned. She looked really angry

—which was silly, as Nelly said later, since ninety cents was all there was, so there wasn't any use her trying to get a dollar out of them.

"I have five cents," said Rose suddenly. She reached into her skirt pocket and took it out. "I think you should let us have it for that," she added firmly in her most grown-up tone. "After all, you don't have to deliver it."

The woman, still frowning, thought this over a minute. Then she gave a nod. She turned and went back into the house. They heard a great fluttering and squawking, and presently she came around the corner of the porch carrying a very upset frizzly chicken by its feet.

Nelly was so excited and so relieved to get the chicken that her hands shook as she counted out the money. Rose added her nickel and after thanking the woman—"though I don't know what for!" Callie said later. "She was just downright hateful and she told a lie, too!"—they hurried back to the hot, sunny road.

"Whew!" said Rose. "I'm glad to get out of that place. I haven't been to Crawdad for years, and it will be a long time before I go back. It's real spooky there."

"I wonder what makes it seem that way?" asked Callie.

Nelly was struggling with the frizzly. Its body felt hot and far too thin, and it glared about with its little red eyes as if it were terrified. Two little black feathers near its beak looked like a pair of spectacles. She held it close to her so that it could not get away, and it was like holding a hot potato.

"I think it just seems spooky," Nelly answered, panting a little, "because it's so shady in there under all those trees. And you come into the place after you've been walkin' so long in the glarin' sun."

"And they act so funny," said Callie. "Not comin' to the door, and sayin' they don't have frizzlies. I sure am glad we got one, though."

"Me, too," said Nelly. She felt happy for the first time since she had seen Rena that morning, even though the walk home seemed endless and the sun beat down hotter and hotter.

"What is that funny smell?" asked Rose suddenly.

The three cousins stopped and sniffed the air.

"A polecat?" asked Callie fearfully. It would be awful to meet one out here in the country—or anywhere for that matter.

"No, it doesn't smell exactly like that, but it does a little, too."

"Maybe it's a little polecat," said Nelly, giggling.

"It smells like . . . Oh!" cried Rose. "Look!"

The country around Willow Landing was as flat as a table for miles. As long as a road went straight you could see an object coming along it before it was close enough to tell exactly what it was. But the road that the cousins were on made a sharp curve, and in the bend was a cluster of small chinaberry trees.

As Rose spoke the most amazing apparition came into view. At first they could not believe their eyes. A group of small dark animals spread across the road. There seemed to be about twenty of them the size of big dogs. Behind them moved the strangest wagon or caravan the girls had ever seen. It was like a short flatboat, for it had a base and a sort of a room on top of that. In front of the little room was a seat, and on the seat sat a very old, very dirty, very hairy man. He was dressed in odd pieces of sacking and looked like the pictures of Robinson Crusoe Nell had seen in a book.

The wagon itself was made of wood which had been almost completely covered with patches of tin. Odd pieces stuck out here and there, and the whole was hung with bundles and rags which looked like smaller copies of the raggedy, bundled old man himself. The animals were all tied to the cart in a harness of many ropes and were guided by reins on the two center creatures. There was no doubt what they were, as they and the smell got closer. They were little brown goats as hairy and as dirty as the old man himself. They spread across the entire road and showed no sign of stopping or moving over as they approached the girls. As they came closer the goaty smell became almost unbearable.

The cousins stepped off the roadway into the grass, all three of them holding their noses. The strange cart and its stranger steeds passed by in a

leisurely manner, the little goats walking sedately
until they got to the exact spot where the girls stood
at the side of the road.

Suddenly the frizzly chicken, which Nelly was
holding with only one hand while she held her nose
with the other, flew up into the air and landed on
one of the brown goats.

The goat stopped and then began to prance as
the chicken clung to the thick hair on its back,
squawking loudly. Nelly stood and wrung her
hands, and the cousins stared in horror as the goat
broke its worn rope harness and dashed off into the
cotton patch.

"We've got to get him!" screamed Nelly and started after the leaping-and-bucking animal.

The other two girls followed her but soon gave up the chase as the goat dashed between the rows of cotton and in no time was far beyond their reach.

Nelly ran and ran, zigzagging as the goat cut between the plants, and the cotton pickers shouted and waved their arms.

All this time the old man sat on his odd-looking wagon and just watched, as if he had no interest in the commotion at all.

At last Nelly, winded and heartbroken, stopped

running and just stood there, bawling in the cotton rows. The girls could not hear her, but they could plainly see her mouth wide open in her red face. They knew just how miserable and worried she was.

The goat had stopped running now and was ambling among the rows nibbling first at a boll and then at a leaf. The frizzly chicken had been flung off somewhere along the way and was nowhere to be seen.

"Oh, poor Nelly!" cried Rose, her own eyes filling with tears. "She's lost the frizzly!"

"Yeah, and after payin' all her money for it," said Callie glumly.

"That hateful old goat!" cried Rose, stamping her foot, which only made a soft plop in the dirt. "That hateful, smelly, nasty old goat!"

"Well, it wasn't all his fault," said Callie, looking at the nasty, smelly old man who had turned to stare at them. "The frizzly did jump on him."

The old man kept staring at them. Because of his beard and his long hair and his wrinkles, they could not tell whether he was smiling or frowning. But he looked entirely too much like one of the head-hunters in the big fat yellow volumes of *Wood's Natural History* that Bert owned, to make Callie feel like getting close to him—even if he hadn't smelled so awful.

He reached slowly into the mysterious layers of his ragged clothing and drew out a whistle. He blew on it—two ear-splitting notes—and the goat out in the cotton field raised its head. The old man blew again and this time the goat, after giving a final yank at a cotton boll, came trotting back to the roadside with the boll in his mouth.

The old man got down from the wagon very slowly and stiffly, his rags fluttering and sagging as he moved. He took the goat by the makeshift harness around its neck and shoulders, picked up the broken rope, and tied it back on. Then without a word, he crawled back up on the wagon, flapped the reins of the two lead goats, and the whole crazy-looking bunch of them moved slowly away.

Rose and Callie stared after him a few seconds and then turned back to look at poor Nelly plodding across the cotton fields.

She was still crying bitterly when she reached the road, and the cousins ran to meet her, putting their arms around her and trying to think of something to say that would comfort her.

"Did you see which way the frizzly went?" asked Rose when Nelly's sobs had died out a little.

"No!" cried Nelly and hiccoughed. "I—I—couldn't see him at all for the cotton plants. But I looked and looked all the way back. He's just gone! And now I don't have a frizzly for Rena, and I've spent all my money!"

"Never mind," said Rose, who was always tender-hearted even if she did tease sometimes. "Callie and I will help you get another one."

But Nelly was not to be comforted. The long hot walk to Crawdad and back, the loss of her money and the chicken, the thought of Rena's disappointment, and the fact that the frizzlies were so hard to get anyway, were too much. She stumbled along the road, her head under its sunbonnet, bowed in grief, and her two cousins walked slowly beside her. They looked at her from time to time in sympathy, but were not able to do or say anything to help.

A Daring Escapade

Nelly sat in the porch swing and pushed it back and forth with one bare foot. The sun was hot and bright, but to Nell the whole world looked gloomy. Rena was still "put out" with her because Natchez had eaten her pet chicken, and that awful trip to Crawdad the other day to get another frizzly had been a terrible failure. On top of that, the River Queen had had three kittens and Nell's mother had said some of them must go!

"Eleven cats are simply more than I can stand!" she had cried. "You'll have to give some of the older ones away."

The trouble was that Nell had given cats to

everybody in the neighborhood. Sometimes the cats came back. Sometimes, Nell suspected, the children to whom she had given them secretly brought them back themselves. She could think of no one who would take one of her cats, and the aunts had muttered dreadful words, like "drowning" and "taking them away," which to Nell meant just that—taking them far out into the country to let them fend for themselves.

As Uncle Doctor pointed out, that wasn't so bad, because there were always shrimp and small fish, turtle eggs, and other things to eat, and lizards and frog for them to catch. And the whole Mississippi to drink from!

But to Nelly it was unthinkable that a kitten should not have an owner. Nobody to curl up on the bed with on a rainy day or a cold night, nobody to pet it when it had been frightened by dogs, nobody to admire it when it danced on its hind legs or sprang like a tiger at a grasshopper . . . In other words, nobody to love and cherish it—that was no life for a cat! She simply must find homes for them.

Natchez came flying around the house and stopped under the pecan tree. He looked very angry, and his fur was sparkling with drops of water. He shook first one foot and then the other, holding his legs straight out as if he could not bear to feel them. Then he sat down and began to wash himself thoroughly.

Nelly knew what had happened. Rena had thrown a dipperful of water on him.

"I got to break him of gettin' after my chickens," Rena had explained. "There ain't nothin' a cat hates like water. It don't hurt him, but it'll sure break him. An' I mean for him never to eat my chickens —not of *no* kind—again!"

Nelly got up and went out to the barn. Memphis Belle lay in the loft window, sleeping. Her four kittens were playing up and down the ladder to the loft, and one of them came and looked out of the window as Nelly came toward the barn. In an old feed bin the River Queen lay with her three new kittens, two black and one yellow, and from a wheelbarrow the lovely Rosalie, all cream-and-white with blue eyes, looked up and mewed. Nell picked her up, and hugging her, sat down in the wheelbarrow with her feet hanging over.

Could she bear to part with Memphis Belle's kittens? Could she give away Rosalie with her sweet round face and lovely thick fur? Nobody wanted

Natchez; he was old and showed the scars of battle.
But it was harder to give away one like Rosalie who
had lived here all her life.

It would simply have to be Memphis Belle's kittens, Nelly thought resignedly.

But I can't do it. They always cling to me and
mew so! I'll get Bert and Benjy to do it. I'll give
them the new paint box Mamma brought me from
Natchez.

Mamma had meant the paint box for Nell's birthday, but when she heard about the frizzly and the
trip to Crawdad, she had given it to Nell then to
comfort her.

Giving up the paint box was almost as bad as
parting with the kittens. The whole thing was so

sad that Nelly decided to get it over with at once. She left the barn and went over to Aunt Cara's house where she found Bert and Benjy playing mumbletypeg in the back yard.

Ten minutes later the boys went off with two baskets and two kittens in each basket. Nelly went into the house and crawled under the dining-room table, where she could weep and no one would think of looking for her. It was dark and warm in the dining room and presently she cried herself asleep.

It was almost suppertime when Nell woke to hear Bert calling her. She was stiff, and her eyes felt heavy. But she came out from under the table and went to meet him in the hall.

"We gave 'em all away," said Bert smugly. "Pierre and Jean took one. They said they'd feed it all the shrimp it could eat—so *it'll* be happy. We gave two to a river-boat family that are goin' to Natchez to live. They said they heard there were lots of rats and mice at Natchez-under-the-Hill, where they're going to tie up. And we gave one to a feller that was shopping at Wang Lee's. He said his little girl out in the country had been beggin' for one for a long time. And now where's the paint box?"

Nelly went into her bedroom. She was stiff and

sore from crying so hard and from sleeping on the floor and she wanted to get rid of Bert and Benjy as soon as she could.

From the desk which Uncle Judge had given her for her birthday a year before, she took the paint box. It was brand-new and the colors looked lovely in their fresh, tidy cakes—especially the deep blue and Crimson Lake. The brushes lay neat and clean in the little grove at one side, and the inside of the black box was clean and shining. She hoped her mother would understand.

Tears blurred Nelly's eyes, so that the colors all ran together. But Bert didn't see them. His eyes were glued on the box.

"Gee!" he said, breathing the licorice they had bought at Wang Lee's. "Gee, Nell, it's a beauty."

Benjy, too, was goggle-eyed. They took the box and walked out of the house, gabbling about what they were going to do with it, arguing about which brush belonged to which boy.

Nelly sat down in the chair by the window and stared out into the yard. Her kittens were gone. Her new paint box was gone. She'd never even had a chance to try it! Her dollar was gone. The frizzly from Crawdad Row was gone. Outside, the sun was setting and it was deathly still except for the

mournful sound of a wood dove's cooing. Nelly
felt as though she were alone in all the world and
that nothing—nothing pleasant or nice or exciting
would ever happen to her again.

She was still sitting there, wiping an occasional
tear away, when she heard someone shouting her
name in the hall. She had been so lost in her own
troubles that she had almost forgotten where she
was. She sprang up so suddenly that she turned
over the chair she was sitting in, and ran to her bedroom door.

The hall was almost dark, but against the open
front doorway she saw Callie and Rose.

"Listen!" cried Callie. "We know where there's
a frizzly chicken!"

"You do? Oh, where?" asked Nelly.

"Old Mrs. McBroom has one," said Callie.

"But she won't sell it," added Rose, and Nelly's
face fell.

"What good does it do me to know about it
then?" she asked, all her mournfulness returning.

"It's going to set someday, she thinks," said Rose.
"Anyway, it's laid two or three eggs and she says
if it sets before the eggs spoil, she'll give you a little
frizzly."

Nelly stood still, thinking this over. It might be

a week or two before the frizzley set; then it would be several weeks before the baby frizzly would be big enough to give away—months, maybe. And all that time Rena would be mad at her and at her cats, and Nelly herself would be unhappy, waiting and waiting.

"Why can't Mrs. McBroom set her right away?" she asked.

"Because, silly, you can't just set a hen!" cried Rose. "They set themselves—I think."

"Did anybody ever try to set one?" asked Nelly, suddenly excited. "I bet they never did. Then how do they know? Listen—" she lowered her voice, and the other two drew closer in the dim hall—"let's get that frizzly hen and bring her over to our barn *and set her!*"

"But that would be stealing!" cried Rose, shocked.

"It wouldn't, either," said Nelly. "We'd just be borrowing it. And certainly we can borrow a little old hen if it's going to make Rena happy."

"Sure," agreed Callie. "It's not gonna hurt the old thing."

"Tomorrow we'll slip over there and get that hen ——" began Nelly.

"Why not tonight?" asked Callie. "It'll be roostin' then. Old Broom's henhouse is right on the back road. We could slip in there right after dark and get her and bring her over here. Then when she lays another egg we'll set her—and whoopee! We'll have Rena her frizzly!"

Just then the big dinner bell at Rose's house began ringing.

"Come on, we've got to go to supper," said Rose. "Now remember, we have to act as if we're not even *thinking* about a frizzly."

The grown-ups were rocking and talking on Uncle Judge's porch when the dusk deepened into darkness. The children were all out in the road playing hide-and-seek, so nobody thought anything of it when they disappeared occasionally.

Mrs. McBroom lived just down the road, and it was a matter of seconds to run across the grassy lots and slip around behind her chicken house. The boys had been let in on the secret so that they wouldn't come yelling after the girls and scare the chickens.

It was quite dark in the chicken house and Rose, giving a disgusted sniff, said she'd stand outside and keep watch.

"There are just two roosts," whispered Callie. "I'll take one and you take the other. We'll feel each

chicken, and when we come to the frizzly we'll
grab it. We'd better put a hand over its beak so it
won't squawk, too."

The girls crept inside the hot, smelly little building and began to feel along the dirty roosts. The
sleepy chickens growled and muttered but made no
outcry. Nelly talked softly to each one and then said
suddenly, "I've got her! This is the frizzly!"

"Shhh!" said Callie. "You want the old Broom
to hear you?"

Nelly, clutching the poor frizzly around its head,
held it fast in both arms. The girls hurried back
across the lots and into Nelly's barn.

"We'll have to shut it up in something tonight,"
said Nelly, fumbling around in the dark. "What
about one of the empty corncribs?"

"Fine, just so one of the cats isn't in it," said Rose.

Nelly paled at the thought. Suppose she shut
in Mrs. McBroom's frizzly with the River Queen
and her kittens or even Memphis Belle? That
would be two frizzlies gone to a horrible fate, and
two frizzlies to replace!

"Feel around in there," she said to Rose, and see
if there's a cat on the bottom."

"Not me!" said Rose promptly. "There might be
a rat."

"Yeah," agreed Callie, "or a possum or a gopher."

"Well, how am I gonna know?" wailed Nelly. "I can't see!"

"Where's the lantern Asa keeps out here?" asked Rose.

"It's hanging over by that door," said Nell. "And there are some matches in the tin can beside it."

After some stumbling and fumbling Rose found the lantern and the matches.

"Shut the barn door, Callie," ordered Nell. "We don't want Rena or somebody to see a light out here. Keep the light low, Rose. I just need enough to see by. Here, hold it over the bin. Goody! It's empty. Here you go, Mrs. Frizzly."

She plopped the small hen down into the bin and closed the top with a bang.

"I'll bring her some food and water in the morning," she said. "And as soon as she lays an egg we'll set her."

The lantern out, they hurried back to their game and nobody except the children knew that a crime had been committed—Mrs. McBroom's frizzly had been hen-napped.

Perhaps the move was a shock to her; perhaps Mrs. Frizzly didn't like being in a dark bin, but whatever the cause, it was two days before she laid an egg.

The girls were excited beyond words. They spent the morning building a nest. There were plenty of wooden boxes in the barn and plenty of hay. They made it extra soft and put the small unlovely look-ing egg in the middle of it. Then they waited for the frizzly to set.

"She's just not going to," said Nell after they had hung over the edge of the bin for nearly half an hour. "We'll have to put her on it."

That wasn't so hard, although it isn't easy to catch a nervous frizzly chicken when you're hanging headfirst into a deep corncrib. But to keep her on the nest was another thing. Every time Nell set the chicken upon the soft hay and took her hands away, Mrs. Frizzly leaped up and ran around the floor of the bin, shrieking.

"She's going to bring Rena or your mother out here," said Rose, "making all that racket. We've got to think of some way to make her stay on the nest and be quiet."

The girls stood and stared at the frizzly for some time, and then Nell said, "Wait a minute."

She went out of the barn and came back presently with a saucepan lid and a ball of string.

"Lift that nest out," she said to Callie, "and be careful of the egg!"

Callie lifted the nest out and set it on top of a closed feed bin.

Nelly captured Mrs. Frizzly and set her on the nest.

"Now, Callie, you set that lid over the nest, and Rose you take the string and tie it on. It'll cramp her a little, but if she won't set, it's her own fault. Maybe after she's been here a day or so she'll like it."

"But how can she eat and drink?" cried Rose.

"I'll have to come out here and let her off a couple of times a day, I suppose," said Nell, sighing. Hatching a frizzly was going to be no easy job, she could see, but she would do almost anything to make up to Rena for losing her pet.

The frizzly was at last safely tied under the lid. One indignant red eye peered out at them, and she seemed to be muttering to herself about what she thought of the whole arrangement. But there was no doubt about one thing. Mrs. Frizzly had been set, and she was going to keep on setting—at least for a while.

The Storm

For two days Nelly went out to the barn and let poor Mrs. Frizzly out for a few minutes in the morning and evening. She got Callie to go with her and help put the chicken back on the nest, since she found she could not hold the frizzly and tie the cord, too.

Meanwhile, there was an exciting feeling of danger, for it looked as though their plans might be discovered.

Mrs. McBroom was asking all over the neighborhood for her frizzly, and she finally decided that one of Nell's cats must have eaten it. She came to call on Nelly's mother and what she had to say made all the aunts look very upset.

"If I find that one of those cats has eaten Mrs.

McBroom's chicken," said her mother to Nell, "you will have to get rid of them—*all* of them!"

Poor Nelly!

"What shall I do?" she asked her cousins. "If I tell Mamma I have the frizzly, she'll punish me; I know she will. And if she decides the cats ate it, I'll l–lose all my darling cats!"

"She can't *prove* that a cat ate it," Rose pointed out. "Maybe she won't do anything for a while, and by that time the little frizzly will be hatched."

But it looked as if Nelly's luck was still bad. The very next day she came down with a sore throat and was put to bed. Besides feeling miserable, Nelly had the terrible worry of what would happen to Mrs. Frizzly while she was laid up.

At last she thought of asking Bert and Benjy to take care of her. "Please do it for me," she pleaded. "I'll do something for you sometime, honest I will."

To the boys, taking care of a secretly captured chicken was a fine game. Before they got tired of it Nell was well enough to take over.

And then it began to rain. It rained and it rained and it rained and it RAINED!

Nelly and Callie stood by the window in Nelly's parlor and stared out at the rain.

"Four whole days!" grumbled Nelly. "Just rain,

rain, rain! If it's not gonna stop, I wish it would do something else—blow up a hurricane or something. Just rain is too stupid."

"Well, it gave Miss Fink pneumonia, so we don't have to begin school," said Callie, "and if it keeps on, the river'll rise and get over the levee and then we'll have a flood."

"We've never had a real big flood that I can remember," said Nell. "Oh, I wish we would!"

"What would we do?" asked Callie. "Would we get a boat and row off somewhere? Or would we have to swim? I can't swim," she added, looking a little anxious.

"I don't know," answered Nelly. "But I wish we'd have one. At least it would give us something to do!"

"You would not say that if you had ever been in a flood," said Missmamma, who sat by the window with her mending. "It is a terrible thing to see your home swept away and broken to pieces by wind and water. Everything you own can be destroyed: your pets and livestock drowned, sometimes even members of your family killed, and the very ground where your home has stood can be washed away by the river. I hope I never see another bad flood!"

The children said nothing for a minute or two. Nelly thought of her home being whirled away by the angry river, of her family fighting for their lives in the muddy water, and her poor cats and their kittens drowned! And, oh, the poor frizzly! She would have to let it go! It was a horrible picture.

"Well, maybe just a little storm," she said presently. "Just something to look at."

Missmamma smiled. "Often we get what we wish for, and then we wish we hadn't."

Nelly continued to look gloomy, and Missmamma added, "We don't usually have a bad flood at this time of year—a hurricane, maybe, or a rise in the river. But the real floods come in the spring. I hope I never see another at any time of year!" she added.

That afternoon Nelly remembered Missmamma's words. For the wind began to rise and it blew harder and harder. Trees bent to the ground. The sky grew so black that Missmamma and Aunt Fanny had to light the lamps, and Rena sat in the kitchen shivering, for she was terrified of storms. The big pecan by the front porch twisted and groaned, and one great limb broke off and came crashing down right in front of the house.

Grass and leaves blew across the three yards of the cousins' houses and the chickens in the back yard were swept before the wind so that their feet barely touched the ground. A chicken coop skittered across the yard and broke to pieces against the smokehouse. A man was driving a cartload of furniture down the road when suddenly piece after piece was lifted off and blown into the fields. He had to stop his horse and go chasing after it, trying to hold his hat on with one hand and dragging the chairs and tables with the other.

Even Nelly worried a little, but she soon forgot it in the excitement of the storm. She loved the darkness, the howling wind, the strange look of all the outdoors, with its wild movement and the flying objects. What was happening to her cats and the frizzly bothered her a little, but they had all been in the barn when the storm broke and she felt sure they were safe. The cats would crouch down in the heavy feed bins or bury under the hay and be warm and cozy.

Just before suppertime Uncle Doctor stopped at the house. He put his horse in the barn and came in the back door, leaning against the wind. Rain ran off his hat and coat in streams and made a puddle around him on the kitchen floor. "The river's rising,

Fanny," he told Nell's mother. "I think we'd all better move over to Judge's for the night."

"Oh, dear!" said Miss Fanny, looking about at her precious house. "Do you really think we'll have a flood, John?"

"Can't tell," said Uncle Doctor. "If this keeps up, anything can happen. Better be prepared, anyway."

"Well," said Nell's mother, "we'll keep Callie and Missmamma for supper, and then we'll all go over as soon as we can get our things together. Do you think we should move anything?"

"You won't have time," said Uncle Doctor. "Not tonight, anyway. And if it doesn't flood, you won't need to. I think we're safe from high water tonight, but this wind is dangerous. If the river is still rising tomorrow, I'll get some of the pickers to help you get up the rugs and move the books and things. We're fortunate that here we have miles of open space for the water to spread out. It's the river itself that could hurt us."

Nelly wondered what he meant. If the river wasn't water, what was it? And if it was going to spread out over the miles of flat cotton fields, how could it do much harm—to houses, that is?

She asked her mother as they ate supper and talked over great rolls of deafening thunder and the sound of wind tearing at the house.

"Uncle Doctor means that if the river washes away any of the land, we'd be in real danger. The house could go, and the barn. The river has often changed its course and wiped out whole towns. But that hasn't happened in years," she added as Nelly's eyes grew round with fright and Callie choked on her buttered biscuit. "We're only going to Uncle Judge's because there is more room, and if the lower floor did flood, we could go upstairs."

It was a strange evening. The girls helped the older women gather up clothes and extra blankets, for it was turning cold. Nell's mother moved several things she especially loved—some of her books, her best dresses, and the family photograph album—to the top of the piano or upon shelves. Nelly began to understand how dreadful a flood could be. Suppose the water came into the house and rose higher and higher, covering the lovely flowered rug in the parlor, soaking the books so that they swelled and came to pieces, warped the piano, and swirled around breaking dishes and ornaments!

If it did that, it would certainly drown all the

cats. And poor Mrs. Frizzly, tied down and help-
less, would suffer a horrible death. Nelly wished
with all her heart she could think of an excuse to go
out to the barn and let the little chicken go. She
wished, too, that she had never wished for a flood.

Wrapped up like mummies, they staggered over
to Aunt Rosalie's where Aunt Cara, Uncle Doctor,
and the others had gathered. The yard and the road
were already ankle-deep in water and the wind blew
so hard that it made them stagger. It was good to be
inside where the warm firelight and the bright
lamps shut out the wet and the fierce darkness.

The family gathered around the fire and talked
excitedly about the wind.

"Blew the roof off John Mason's barn," said
Uncle Judge, carefully cutting the end off his cigar.
"Tree down in the churchyard, too, I noticed. If this
keeps up, there's bound to be a lot of damage."

"The worst thing about a wind like this," said
Uncle Doctor, "is that there's so little we can do to
protect ourselves. I only pray I don't get called out
tonight, though this weather is sure to bring on
accidents."

There was more talk, all about storms and floods.
At nine o'clock the girls went up to Rose's room and
sat on her big bed still talking. The three of them

would sleep cozily in it that night, only a little
uneasy about the storm outside.

"I do hope the kittens are safe," said Nelly,
pulling aside the shade and staring out at the darkness. She couldn't see a thing really, because the
night was black and the rain ran down the pane in
a solid sheet of water.

"Of course, they are," said Rose. "The water's not
deep, and they're all holed up in the barn, snug as
bugs in rugs."

"I'm cold!" said Nell, turning away from the
window with a shiver. She rolled over onto the bed
and pulled a big soft quilt over her.

"Let's go to bed," cried Rose. "We'll be warmer
there and we can talk and listen to the storm. Or
we can tell ghost stories."

As if to prove that it would be worth listening
to, the storm gave a sudden spurt, shutters banged,
the wind whined and sobbed, and trees brushed
against the house like the reaching claws of giant
animals. Callie gave a little scream and jumped
upon the bed beside Nelly.

"Come on," urged Rose. "Let's get undressed."

In a few minutes they were in their long night-
gowns, and Callie and Nell were snuggled close together in bed.

"I wonder what they're doing downstairs?" asked Callie, thinking of Benjy and Bert perhaps still by the fire with the grown-ups.

"I don't know," said Rose, "but I bet they're having something to eat. Mamma made some doughnuts yesterday. I'm going to go down and get us some."

The idea of lying in a warm bed, munching doughnuts while the storm outside blew and moaned, seemed wonderful to the cousins. Rose put on her slippers and went out into the hall. Even with all the doors and windows shut she could feel a slight draft. She hurried down the back stairs to the kitchen. Rena and Lizzie, their own cook, were

sitting close to the coal stove, sipping coffee and talking of terrible storms they remembered.

Rose found the doughnuts in a big bread bowl.
Taking six of them, she hurried back upstairs. She
handed the doughnuts out, blew out the lamp, and
hopped into bed. What fun! They lay there contentedly, munching and talking. The wind howled
and rattled things, and the rain came down in a
gusty roar.

But at last the little girls slept, warm and full
and happy.

It rained for three more days. The river rose and
slipped over the levees, spreading out over the yards,
the roads, and the big cotton fields as far as you
could see.

It was fun, all of them being in one house, at
least for the first two days. But Nelly was worried
about her cats. What were they eating? Had they
tried to swim away? Were some of them drowned?
Had the frizzly starved to death? Oh, if only she
could get over to the barn without giving her secret
away! If she told of the frizzly, she would have to
return it and Rena would never have one.

When the rain stopped two days later she begged
to go home, but the water was still as high as Nell's

knees. Besides, the soft black mud was treacherous. Uncle Doctor said he would try to get over there.

He laid planks across the yard, making a path from one edge of Missmamma's flower beds to the other. The flower beds were bordered with rocks which kept the planks above water in most places. Then, Uncle Doctor, looking like the tightrope walker on the *Floating Palace,* tiptoed across the planks to the stable. A little later he came out riding Ned, his faithful old buggy horse. Nelly watched him go out to the road and over to her house.

Would he go into the barn and find all the cats and the frizzly drowned, limp and soaking wet and horrible? Nell thought she could not wait until he came back, and yet she dreaded to hear the awful truth.

Her mother and Aunt Cara had given him a list of food and clothes to bring back, and just when Nell thought she couldn't bear it any longer, he came riding in again. He had so many bags and boxes and bundles strapped onto himself and old Ned that all the aunts and cousins watching from the windows began to laugh.

They ran to the back door to help him unload and Nell cried, "My cats! How are my cats, Uncle Doctor?"

"Better than ever," he said, puffing a little as he carried in the bundles. "One of 'em's had kittens."

"Oh! Rosalie's had her kittens!" cried Nell, clapping her hands. "Hers are always the loveliest."

Nell was delighted, but her mother groaned and threw up her hands.

"They've got to go!" she said.

"It would be a good time to drown them," said Uncle Doctor, but Nell gave such a cry of horror that he said no more except, "I fed 'em all."

"I'll give them away," Nell promised. "I'll find *somebody* who wants them."

Oh, dear! She still didn't know what had happened to the frizzly, and she didn't dare ask.

I wonder if anybody else gets into the awful messes that I do? thought Nelly miserably.

Poor Frizzly! Poor Nelly!

All night Nelly tossed and dreamed about the poor captured frizzly. If only she hadn't tied it down, perhaps it could have gotten out and found some food. But if it had gotten out, it would either have drowned or in some way reached Mrs. McBroom's and then, of course, Nelly would have to start all over again in her effort to replace Rena's pet.

Nelly woke up and worried some more; then dropped off to sleep to dream that she was the frizzly and that Callie was a large black cat which sat beside her and said, "The water is rising! The water is rising and we'll all be drowned!"

When she woke very early that morning she felt as if she had walked for miles and had had no sleep at all. She sat up and looked around the big bed-

room. It looked so peaceful it was hard to think that
she had had such awful dreams there.

But it wasn't really peaceful, for even now that
she was awake her worries continued. Suddenly she
made up her mind. There was only one thing to be
done. She would have to risk being punished and
wade through the mud and rescue the frizzly.

She got out of bed and dressed quietly so as not
to wake Rose or Callie. She'd go barefoot and hope
the mud wasn't deep enough to get on her clothes.

She crept downstairs. It was strange to know
that everyone else in the house was asleep. The
halls were dim and cold and the rooms full of un-
familiar shadows.

Nelly tiptoed out through the kitchen and un-
bolted the back door. The water had gone down a
little, but the mud looked thick and slippery as
though somebody had poured a great bowl of fudge
all over the countryside. She stepped off the back
steps and set her foot down in the brown goo. It
sank several inches, and she clutched the post of the
porch desperately. Then she took a step. Ugh! It
was horrible! A little mud to squinch your toes in
was one thing, but slimy, cold deep mud that came
almost halfway up your legs and held onto you like
a terrapin, was something else.

Nelly pulled up one foot and looked to make sure all of it had come out of the mud. Surely some of it must have stuck there, she thought, from the way it felt. She put one foot down again gingerly and drew up the other. The mud made a sickening, sucking sound. Gosh, much more of that and she'd wake up everybody in the house!

Step by step, wavering and staggering, pulling and slipping, she made her way slowly across Uncle Judge's yard. Now she had to go through Uncle Doctor's yard, and then she'd be right at her own barn. Her legs were beginning to ache. The mud had splashed her dress and twice she had lost her

balance and had fallen forward, thrusting her arms
into the deep smelly stuff.

"Boy, will I catch it when Mamma sees me!" she
muttered. But nothing would have made her turn
back. She was almost there now, and the thought of
the suffering frizzly kept her going.

She wished she had brought Callie with her, but
that would only have gotten her cousin in trouble
and heaven knows, thought Nelly, I've got trouble
enough!

At last she crawled through the place in her
own fence where two boards were missing and in
another moment she stood at the barn door.

The barn smelled musty and it was filled with a
watery, faint light. Up on the rafters sat Memphis
Belle and as soon as Nelly called to her, heads began
to appear from bins and hen nests. It was wonderful
to see them all well and only a little distressed by
the water. Nelly wished she could see the new kittens, but she knew the mother would have taken
them to the loft, and it was the frizzly Nell had
come to see about. So she promptly waded across
the barn floor to the bin where she had left the poor
thing.

She hated to open the lid and look in. Would she

find a sodden mass of feathers, a frail heap of damp
bones, or just a dead, stiff chicken? She felt a little
sick as she bit her lower lip and raised the lid.

The bin had been built upon a rack a foot or so
above the floor, and the first thing that Nelly
noticed was that there was no water in it, only
dampness on the bottom. Well, Mrs. Frizzly hadn't
drowned anyway. She bent over and began to untie
the saucepan lid. She could see the little chicken's
head now. It drooped to one side as if the frizzly
were dead. Nelly moaned. She imagined herself
having to bury it and confess to Mrs. McBroom that
she had let it die.

Or else I'll have to carry this guilty secret all my
life, she thought, and I'll pine away and die and
nobody will know what killed me. They'll wonder
why I am so pale and wan and why I get thinner
and thinner . . . she had got the lid untied now and
she stopped thinking of herself to stare at the
frizzly.

It was alive. That was one thing she could be
glad of. But it certainly looked strange. Its head
was all to one side, and it didn't try to get out of the
nest. Maybe she likes it now, thought Nelly hopefully. Missmamma says you can get used to any-

thing. Or maybe the poor thing's too weak from hunger to move! she added to herself in horror.

She picked up the nest and the frizzly and moved them over to the bench where Asa worked on the harnesses. She set the nest down and stood staring at the frizzly, but it still made no move.

"She's probably starving," muttered Nelly, and plunged through the mud to a feed bin where she grabbed up a handful of oats. She sprinkled them on the bench, and said, "Chick-chick-chick!" in a coaxing voice.

But the frizzly simply sat and stared in a sad one-sided way.

Nelly brushed the grain around with a muddy hand. "Come on and get it, stupid!" she said impatiently, because she was frightened. Suppose the frizzly was too weak to stand up and suppose it was too late to save it!

She picked up the little chicken and was shocked to find it as light as the little bundle of bones she had been afraid she might see in the bin. She stood it on its feet, but the poor frizzly had been tied down so long with its legs crossed that it could only flop down on the bench whenever Nelly picked it up.

"Great jumpin' rattlesnakes, I've *ruined* her!" groaned Nelly. "Come on, Mrs. Frizzly, eat some of this stuff! *Please,* Mrs. Frizzly!"

She held some of the oats in her hand and after a moment the little chicken pecked at it feebly.

I reckon she's awful thirsty, too, thought Nelly, and setting the chicken down she scooped up some dirty water in a rusty pan. This seemed to be just what the frizzly wanted, for it began to drink at once, holding its head up on its crooked neck as best it could.

When it had drunk its fill the frizzly began to peck at the oats hungrily. Nelly felt the load of her worries lifting as the chicken ate more and more and its legs and neck began to unbend.

Maybe she'll live after all, Nell thought hopefully.

When the frizzly's craw was sticking out like a pincushion, it stopped eating and sat down, cross-legged. It glared at Nelly as if to say, "A fine thing! Leaving me here to starve and get a permanent bend in my legs!" Its red eye looked at Nelly so hard that she moved away.

"Could I help it if we had a flood?" she mumbled. "Now come on, I'm goin' to fix you a nice dry nest, and I'm goin' to put a lot of soft hay in it. I won't tie you down, I'll just shut the bin and you can set or not, whichever you want, till I get back home."

Nelly fixed the nest and set the pan of water in one corner of the bin. Then she poured a big pile of oats in the other. She had a feeling that it might be a good while before she could get out to the barn again.

Then she went back, slogging through the thick mud, and got the frizzly. She set the hen down in the bin and shut the lid. She was about to leave when she remembered the old nest. I'd better throw that out and hide the lid, she thought. If I don't, somebody's sure to notice it.

She waded back and picked up the nest. There was something queer in it. It was . . . it couldn't be . . . but it was! A new, rather small white egg!

Nelly nearly fell flat, hurrying over to the feed bin with the egg clutched in her hand. She opened the bin again and, leaning over, laid the egg gently on the fresh hay.

"Good old frizzly!" she said softly. "You're trying, aren't you? Now you lay some more and then you set on 'em, hear? And I won't ever let you go without feed and water again!"

She was feeling quite happy when she waded out of the barn. But it was broad daylight now and, looking down at her muddy hands and dress, Nelly shuddered to think what her mother was going to say when she saw her.

"I'll slip in the back way and get Rena to wash me off, and then I'll sneak upstairs and get a clean dress," she muttered to herself.

But once again Nelly's plans met with disaster.

She had been missed when Callie and Rose got up, and now the whole household was looking for her. Her mother and Missmamma were in the kitchen questioning Rena and Lizzie when Nelly opened the back door.

Missmamma gave a shriek, but Nelly's mother merely stood and stared. And no wonder! Nelly's face was splattered with mud. The hem of her dress was wet and bedraggled. She was muddy up to her knees and her elbows. Miss Fanny looked as if she was not even sure that this was her child.

Needless to say, there was all the trouble and hullabaloo that Nelly had feared. Her mother had Rena bring a tub into the kitchen. They stripped off Nelly's clothes, taking each piece between thumb and finger and dropping it onto the back porch as if she had something catching, like smallpox. They poured water over her and scrubbed her with a sponge and a nailbrush until she burned. Then Callie was sent upstairs for a nightgown.

All this time the aunts and Missmamma were running about like distracted chickens, the uncles were yelling for their breakfasts, and Nelly was sobbing, but no louder than her mother, who kept saying, "This is the last straw! I give up! I never saw such a child! What on earth did you think you were doing? *Oh, I just give up!*"

Just as Nelly had put on her nightgown and Rena was drying her damp hair, Uncle Doctor, his breakfast eaten, came out to the kitchen. He looked at Nelly's scrubbed and tear-stained face, and he looked at all the aunts and his mother-in-law, and he began to laugh.

"I don't see anything funny about it!" snapped Nelly's mother. "She is a disgrace!"

"I only wanted to see about something!" bawled Nelly.

"Of course, she did," said Uncle Doctor. "She really did a very brave, if foolish, thing. You don't realize, Fanny, that this child has a sense of responsibility. She went to take care of her pets, didn't you, dumplin'?" He picked Nelly up.

"I give up!" cried Miss Fanny again. "You and Missmamma spoil her so, how can I ever teach her how to behave? She didn't need to go over there. You had fed those dratted cats. Now put her down.

She's going back to bed, and she's going to stay
there."

Uncle Doctor gave Nelly a hug and set her on her
feet. She flew upstairs, jumped into bed, and buried
her head under the pillow.

Oh, dear! Now she was more wicked than ever.
She hadn't gone to feed her cats, she'd gone only
because she had been cruel and stupid and had
almost let the poor frizzly starve to death. And she
had been wicked to take the frizzly, which didn't
belong to her in the first place. It was dreadful to
see her mother cry and to make Missmamma feel
so bad. Nelly'd made everybody but the uncles late
for breakfast, and Rena and Lizzie had had all that
extra work. Nelly guessed she'd always bring sor-
row to those she loved and gray hairs to her mother's
lovely dark head. Perhaps she had better run away
now and not make any more trouble. After a while
when the household settled down—perhaps when
they were all at breakfast—she'd get up and dress
again and slip away. She'd get on a shanty boat
going down to New Orleans, and they'd never have
to bother with her again. She'd leave a note, con-
fessing about the frizzly and asking Callie and Rose
to take care of the cats.

She was cold and sore from the scrubbing and

worn out from the hard wading through the mud. But as she planned how she would go away to spare the family, she grew warmer and drowsier. And when Rena came up a little later with a plate of hot biscuits and sausage and a glass of milk, Nelly lay sound asleep, curled up like one of her kittens.

Discovered!

The water went down and the sun came out. A brisk wind dried the earth, and soon one could hardly tell that there had been a flood.

Rosalie's new kittens turned out to be some of the cutest that Nelly had ever owned, and she tried hard to keep them in the barn out of her mother's sight. There had been so much cleaning up to do after the flood that Miss Fanny had forgotten her orders to give the cats away.

Mrs. Frizzly seemed to be quite well now, although every now and then her legs crossed and she sat down with a surprised look in her little red eyes. Callie and Nell took her back of the barn every now and then and let her stretch herself and eat weed seeds. There was only one thing wrong. She did not seem to be setting very much.

"I never see her on the nest," complained Nelly. "Whenever I open the bin she's walkin' around."

"I think they all do that," said Callie. "Once I heard Missmamma say they get off for exercise and they know just how long they can stay off before the eggs get cold."

"What happens if the eggs get cold?" asked Nelly.

"They spoil," said Callie. "They don't hatch."

"Maybe we oughta put a hot-water bottle in with 'em," said Nelly.

But Callie said the hen knew what she was doing. "She probably wants to hatch them as much as you do," she added.

Alas! Either Mrs. Frizzly had a frizzly mind as well as feathers, or else she didn't really have her heart in her job. A day or so later, when Nelly opened the bin, she gave a little moan. Callie and the boys, who were with her, leaned over and looked in.

"Phew!" cried Bert, reeling back and holding his nose. He pretended to be overcome and staggered about the barn, snorting and puffing and crying, "Lemme outa here! Phew! Lemme out."

"Shut up, Bert!" cried Nelly fearfully. "You want to have Rena out here, or Mamma?"

Callie leaned over and said, "Whew! What is it?"

"One of the eggs spoiled," said Nelly with dignity. "It's just a little bitty old, bad egg; no need to act like it's something awful. Come over here, Benjy, and get it out for me."

"I don't want to," said Benjy, who had moved over to the open barn door. "It smells awful."

"I never saw such silly boys!" exclaimed Nelly. "Well, I'll get it myself."

She leaned far over the bin. The smell was awful, just as Benjy had said. She held her breath and reached down into the corner where the eggs lay. She had to lean pretty far down to reach them.

Either Mrs. Frizzly thought that Nelly planned to get into the bin with her, or else she had just had enough of all this nonsense. Anyway, she gave a shrill cackle and flew up, scratching Nelly's face as she went by, and shrieking like a banshee, landed on the barn floor.

"Grab her! Grab her, stupid!" cried Nelly to Bert. "Don't let her out the door, Benjy! Grab her!"

For a minute the boys stood there, stunned. Then they began to run after her. Mrs. Frizzly, whose legs were still shaky, staggered about the yard, giving shrieks of anger and fright. The boys began

to yell, and Natchez and Memphis Belle ran up a tree and added their hisses and growls to the confusion.

Nell's mother and Missmamma ran out of the house. Rena stuck her head out of the kitchen window and Uncle Judge, who was coming home to lunch, jumped out of his buggy and came striding into the yard.

"What in heaven's name is going on?" cried Missmamma.

"Why, that's a frizzly!" said Miss Fanny. "It must be the one Mrs. McBroom was looking for. What on earth are you boys doing with it?"

"Yes!" thundered Uncle Judge, who was tall and rather stern looking. "What do you mean chasing

Mrs. McBroom's chicken, and what's it doing over here, anyway?"

Benjy began to bawl, of course, and blurted out that they were only trying to help Nell. Everybody turned to look at Nell, who now wished that the ground would open up and swallow her.

"Help *Nell?*" exclaimed her mother. She set her pretty mouth in a straight line. "Nell, will you please tell me the meaning of this!"

It was a most dreadful occasion. The whole story had to come out. It sounded much worse in the telling.

"It was the same as stealing," Aunt Fanny said, and Nell burst into sobs.

"I believe there is a stiff penalty for stealing livestock," said Uncle Judge, stroking his long mustache. "But I will use all my influence to make your sentence light. You will be tried in my court, you know."

Nelly looked so shocked that Missmamma went and put her arms around her.

"Stop teasing the child, son," she said. "We know you meant no harm, darling," she added, brushing Nelly's hair back from her damp face. "You were trying to do something for Rena. I'm sure that you have learned that whenever you take something that doesn't belong to you—no matter for what reason—it will bring you trouble."

"You must take the frizzly back to Mrs. McBroom and tell her the truth," said Nell's mother.

It was too awful. After all her hopes for getting Rena a pet, after all these weeks of struggling to take care of the frizzly, and after all her worry during the flood, to have to confess her wicked scheme to Mrs. McBroom was just too much.

"Why can't I just let it go home by itself?" asked Nelly miserably. "It's just across the road."

"Because you have done a very wrong thing," said Miss Fanny severely. "You must take the chicken to Mrs. McBroom and tell her that you stole it."

"But I didn't!" cried Nelly. "I just *borrowed* it!"

"Anyway," said Callie bravely, "it wasn't all Nelly's fault. It was me and Rose that thought of it. We told her to."

"Nelly can't grow up doing wrong just because somebody tells her to," said Aunt Fanny.

"But if you are all to blame," said Missmamma, "then you must all go to Mrs. McBroom. Now catch that miserable chicken and go at once. The sooner you get it over with, the sooner you'll feel better."

But even after the girls—including Rose, whose mother was horrified that her ladylike daughter had been mixed up in such a scheme—had gone over to Mrs. McBroom's and had confessed to the frizzly's owner, they didn't feel much better. Mrs. McBroom saw nothing amusing in their efforts to make the frizzly set, and she said a great deal about children who had not been taught right from wrong.

"I feel like a criminal!" said Nelly mournfully as they walked home.

The family, too, was very cold toward them. Only Rena, who now knew how hard they had worked to get her a pet, showed that she loved them. She had hurried out to the kitchen as soon as they left and baked a batch of their favorite crisp spicy cookies. As they sat under the pecan tree, gloomy and upset, she came out with a large bowl of the cookies and glasses of buttermilk. The boys had disappeared lest they be scolded further for helping in the crime, and as Rena sat with her arm around Nelly, the girls poured out the whole story of their search for a frizzly. Rena was so touched that she wept and wiped her eyes on her apron, and in comforting her the girls forgot some of their own woes.

But for a long time a cloud hung over the three houses. Miss Fanny said she despaired of ever making a young lady of Nell. Nell tried so hard to be one that she had no fun at all, and the aunts still acted as though she had led the cousins into mischief when after all, as Nelly told Rose, it had been their idea to take the frizzly.

"Yes," said Rose primly, "but it was your cat that ate Rena's frizzly and if it hadn't been for you, we wouldn't be in all this trouble."

The double first cousins seemed to have turned against her, and Nelly was more miserable than ever. Perhaps, she thought, she had better take herself in hand, try to give up some of her wild, tomboyish ways and learn to be a lady.

Miss Fink got over the pneumonia. School opened, and Nelly learned to parse sentences. She taught Benjy how to remember to spell *geography* by saying *George Edwards' Old Grandfather Rode A Pig Home Yesterday.* She learned "The Charge of the Light Brigade" by heart and how to bound all the states. In fact, she was so good that Uncle Doctor got worried about her and gave her a tonic. It was syrupy and tasted like a rusty dipper.

Christmas came and went and their grandmother in Natchez brought them lovely clothes and marzi-

pan figures of the Christ Child, which they kept
until they were as hard as rocks.

Then there was a long dull winter during which
the cats hardly came out of the barn. Miss Fanny
had almost stopped fussing about them, because
Nelly was so good her mother was worried about
her.

But one day a homely, frightened gray-and-white
creature, which sat up in a tree and yowled most of
the time, came to live with them.

This was the last straw, Nell's mother declared.
"I warn you, Nell," she said sternly, "either you
get rid of some of these cats, or else . . ."

What did "or else" mean? Nelly shuddered to
think!

She was getting desperate when something happened to make her mother forget the cats—at least
for a few days.

The Easter Hat

Easter was early that year, but the aunts had not yet made their spring trip to Natchez to buy the Easter clothes. Two weeks before Easter they set out on the *River Queen*.

Nell's mother had a talk with her before she left. It was all about how Nell simply must keep on trying to be ladylike, learn to take better care of her clothes and try not to be such a tomboy. If this meant not wading in the little creeks made by the river, not climbing the pecan and chinaberry trees, not visiting the shanty-boat people and eating shrimp with Pierre and Jean, and not making mud pies, Nell thought she cared very little for it. But she knew better than to say so.

"I am going to buy you the very prettiest hat and

dress I can find in Natchez," said her mother, kissing Nell's rather unhappy face. "And I hope you'll like them so well that you'll begin to take care of your things."

When they returned, the children went down in Asa's wagon to meet the aunts at the levee. Miss-mamma was driven down in her surrey. At least a dozen large boxes were loaded into the wagon. The girls piled into the surrey, and the boys rode back with Asa, as the aunts were driven to Uncle Judge's house.

As the clothes were being unpacked the girls went into fits of delight over the dainty white dresses, the shiny slippers, the ruffled lacy petticoats, and loveliest of all, the wide-brimmed hats with their ribbons and flowers. Even the boys were impressed with their new pants and jackets and, of course, there were boxes of rich, sweet pralines from Natchez.

Nell's hat was of pale straw with a big bow of pink velvet ribbon. It must truly have been the most beautiful her mother could find, Nell thought, turning it about and looking at it with shining eyes. The crown was covered with pink velvet roses more enchanting than anything she had ever seen. They just matched the sash on her Easter dress.

"Oh, Mamma!" she breathed. "It's so beautiful!"

"Pretty is as pretty does," said Aunt Cara, and almost spoiled it.

After supper the families went to their own homes. Nell carried her beautiful new clothes to her room and put them away—the lovely under-clothes in a special drawer, her dress on a hanger in the wardrobe.

But where could she put the hatbox, she wondered. There was no shelf big enough for it, so at last she decided to slip it under her bed. Twice

before she went to sleep she got out of bed, dragged the big box out and sat looking at the lovely, lovely ribbons and roses. Surely, thought Nell, she would take care of this hat! She would never do anything to spoil it. Anybody could enjoy being ladylike in something as beautiful as this.

The Easter clothes had come on Tuesday, and on Friday Nell's mother said, "Nell, you've done nothing about getting rid of those cats. Now I want you to take this morning to go around and find homes for them. The cousins can help you. And I want those cats out of here by this afternoon!"

"*All* of them?" cried Nell wildly.

"Most of them," said her mother. "You may keep two."

Poor Nell! She felt as if the end of the world had come.

She knew that her mother had good reason to want to get rid of the cats. They fought under the house and kept people awake. When they came indoors they brought fleas that got into the furniture. They tore the lovely fabrics on the chairs and sofas, and they jumped up on the beds and tables with their dusty feet. Once Memphis Belle had dragged a fine fresh fish off the table and out into the yard right behind Rena's back.

"It's not that I mind giving them away so much," Nell told her cousins that morning. "But if I can't find anybody to take 'em, what's going to happen to 'em?"

"We'll drown 'em!" said Benjy happily.

Nell gave him a hard smack and he began to bawl.

"Crybaby!" said Nell, who was ready to cry over the cats herself. "You can't stand being slapped just a little bit, and then you talk about drowning a cat!"

"Yes, you ought to be ashamed of yourself!" said Callie. "Now you just get busy and find one of these cats a nice home!"

So Benjy, sniveling, set off lugging one of the kittens, and Bert, who certainly didn't want to get slapped by Nelly, took Rosalie and another kitten. Nell would not watch him go. Rosalie, with her sweet round face and pink velvet nose, had always been one of her favorites. The girls set out, too, and Nell carried the most recently acquired gray-and-white cat—who fought and scratched and seemed suddenly to weigh as much as a bushel of potatoes.

They went from house to house and from store to store. The trouble was that there were only a few houses in Willow Landing and even fewer stores.

A man at the warehouse down by the levee took two cats. Wang Lee, whose big yellow cat had disappeared since the flood, took Memphis Belle, and a friend of Pierre and Jean's took a kitten on his flatboat which was heading for New Orleans. But not another cat could they get rid of.

At lunch that day, Nell's mother said that as long as all the children were really trying to find homes for Nell's cats, she would give Nell a few more days.

"But get rid of that horrible gray-and-white thing next," she said. "I don't know where it came from, but it comes into the house every time anybody opens a door, and I just won't have it in here. It's the homeliest cat I ever saw," she added.

Poor thing! thought Nelly. It was bad enough to be lost and frightened and to want to live in somebody's house, without people talking so dreadfully about you. She would try to find it a really good home.

But though she tramped from one end of Willow Landing to the other and even out on Crawdad Row, nobody wanted a homely gray-and-white cat. Nelly hoped her mother would forget about it.

Every day and at night before she went to bed, Nelly took out the lovely new hat and looked at the roses. She tried it on and decided that she must brush her wild curls more often. They must look just right on the day she wore the beautiful hat.

On the Thursday afternoon before Easter, she lay on her bed, thinking of how she would look in it.

She would look more grown-up than Rose. People would turn and say, "Who is that stunning young girl? What a beauty she will be in a few years!"

Nell got up from the bed and pulled out the hat-box.

She knelt beside the box and stared. Something *dreadful* had happened to the Easter hat! Where the lovely crown of roses had been, there was a

gray-and-white heaving mass, and instead of the lovely petals of the flowers, there, staring up at her, was a homely, flat cat's face.

Nell saw all this, but she could not believe it. The gray-and-white cat, looking uglier and more dingy than ever, lay right on top of the lovely, lovely hat, and with her were three scrawny gray-and-white newly born kittens. They sprawled all over the hat's brim. The roses were hopelessly crushed, the brim was marked with dirty footprints, and the whole hat was an unbelievable mess! Nelly stared at the scene in horror.

Slowly, what had happened dawned on poor Nell's mind. The old gray was a mother cat. And she had had her kittens in the worst place in the world to choose—in Nell's beautiful new hat! On her knees Nelly rocked back and forth and wept.

After a while, still sobbing, she climbed up on the bed. What would her mother say? It was enough to have such a lovely hat spoiled. But to be scolded for letting it get spoiled and to have one more thing that her mother could hold against the cats—that was just going to be too much!

After a long while Nelly got up and looked in the hatbox again. Maybe it had all been a bad dream. But there lay the cat looking snug and comfortable beside the kittens, and there lay the hat—completely ruined.

Nell went slowly out of the room and up the hall to her mother's room. Miss Fanny lay on her high canopy bed reading a book. She looked very pretty in a white dotted-swiss dressing gown with blue ribbons at the throat. She did not look at all as if she were the mother of a girl whose cat would have kittens in her best hat.

Nell stood in the doorway with one bare foot tucked behind the other. Her mother looked up and saw her daughter's swollen red face. Miss Fanny flung down the book and jumped off the bed, running to Nell and gathering her in her arms.

"Darling! Whatever is the matter?" she cried.

Poor Nell! She burst into sobs and hiccoughs, and all she could say was, "My hat! My . . . *hic* . . . Easter hat!"

The next few minutes were pretty dreadful. Her mother rushed into Nell's room and saw the awful sight.

"That cat!" she cried. "That *horrible* cat! Now look what she's done!"

"She didn't know any better!" wailed Nelly. After all, she thought, if you were going to have babies, wouldn't you pick a lovely bed of roses to have them in? But she knew that it would do no good to tell that to her mother.

It was an afternoon that Nelly always wished she could forget. The hat was ruined beyond repair. It was too late to go to Natchez to get another. "Besides," said her mother tearfully, "that was the only one like it, and almost the last Easter hat they had."

The mother cat was banished to the barn in disgrace, the beautiful hat was burned, and Nelly went to bed unable to swallow a bit of supper.

"You can't go to church without a hat," her mother had said. "You'll have to wear your old blue sailor. I'll put a new ribbon on it, white perhaps."

Nelly could just see herself! A white dress with a pink sash and her faded dark-blue straw with a white ribbon. And Callie and Rose would look like flowers under their dainty wide-brimmed Easter hats. Callie and Rose had cried in sympathy, but they had *their* hats.

On Easter morning the grown-ups tried very hard to act as if nothing was wrong with Nelly's Easter outfit. Missmamma murmured something sympathetic, and Aunt Cara said, "Pretty is as pretty does," in a tone which she meant to be comforting. And after that the subject was ignored. But when they all set out for church in the two surreys, the old blue sailor hat seemed to stand out like a horrible blight in the flower garden of gay, bobbing Easter hats and bonnets. Under it Nell glared at every passer-by, and when she knelt in church her very back bristled with misery and rage.

Afterwards everyone stood outside the church in the lovely spring sunshine, and the ladies in their pretty frocks preened themselves like colorful birds. Nelly felt more than ever like the Ugly Duckling. And it was just then that Tom Broussard—a smart aleck if there ever lived one—stepped up to Nelly and said, "Gosh! Some Easter hat! Where'd you get it? Out of the graveyard?"

"Shut up!" said Bert.

"Who'll make me?" asked Tom, pushing his own new cap onto the back of his head.

He was a handsome boy with thick curly blond hair and big blue eyes. He was much larger than Bert, who now wished he'd said nothing.

"*I'll* make you!" cried Nelly. The blue straw hat was held on by an elastic band. Nelly snatched it from her head, and the band sprang back and stung her chin, which made her madder than ever. Throwing the hat down on the sidewalk, she leaped at Tom—giving him a resounding punch right in the middle of his face—causing him to fall over backward into the gutter. Blood spurted from his nose and upon Nelly, who had thrown herself on him and was now pounding him unmercifully.

Tom's yells and the screams of Callie and Rose brought the grown-ups. Nell's mother shrieked,

Missmamma moaned, Tom's father rushed to pull Nelly away from his howling son. But Uncle Doctor stepped between them and threatened Mr. Broussard with his cane.

"He must have done something to deserve it," Uncle Doctor said. "It's a fair fight, and I'm hoping the best man wins!"

"Stop them!" cried Miss Fanny. "It's disgraceful, right here at the church steps!"

But Uncle Doctor was standing over them with an excited grin on his face.

It only took a moment to defeat Tom. He suddenly bellowed, "I give up!" and rolled over on his face, sobbing into the dust.

Nelly stood up. She did not dare look at her mother and aunts. She walked away stiffly, sure that none of the family would want her to ride with them. Not only had she disgraced them in public, but her lovely new dress was torn and dirty. The sash hung down and trailed along the sidewalk, and the front was bloodstained.

As he watched Nelly walk away Uncle Doctor felt his heart ache for her. He turned to Missmamma and the aunts and said, "Ah, well. Fun's over. Let's go home."

The ladies, frowning and embarrassed, did not

think there had been any fun. They had plenty to say about it until Uncle Doctor said sternly, "The child was provoked into it. She made a good fight, and she's had a lot of disappointments. The Broussard brat had no business to taunt her. Now, not one of you say a word to her! She knows all you'd say, anyway, and she's not to be bothered any further."

"He's right," said Uncle Judge. "The boy deserved to be whipped. I should have liked to hit him, myself!"

The ladies did not look as if they quite agreed, but no more was said about Nelly—at least for a time.

Grandpaw Saves the Day

Nelly wandered down the dusty road toward home, but when she got to the lane to her own house, she turned off. She felt she simply could not face her mother now. After all these months of practicing to be ladylike she had disgraced the family worse than ever. She walked over to the levee and followed the willow path along the river bank. The sun was warm and the river slipping slowly by was soothing. And she needed to be comforted. The cats were still a problem, she had never found a frizzly for Rena, and it began to look as if she would never be anything but a trial to her mother and the aunts.

The Benson's shanty was closed, and only the

hound dog lay on the deck. It wagged a limp tail and rolled sad brown eyes as Nelly went by.

At the next shanty Grandpaw sat asleep in the sun with Coony at his feet. The little creature was sucking on a mussel shell and digging at it with one jet-black finger.

Nelly walked over and sat down on a willow stump. It was so quiet here you could almost hear the silence. Only the water whispering against the muddy bank made any sound. Then Coony sneezed. The sound woke Grandpaw, who sat up and looked at Nelly in surprise.

"Why, howdy, Nell," he said, rubbing a hand over his bristly face. "Whatcha doin' down here— and it Sunday and dinnertime?"

"Nothin'," said Nell glumly.

"Well, you sure picked the right place to do it," said the old man, looking at her shrewdly. "Me an' Coony's been settin' here doin' nothin' for a coupla hours now. Maw and Lallie Bell and the kids done took off with the Bensons to a camp meetin'. Gonna have a baptizin' I hyeered. I woulda gone, but somebody's got to stay here and watch this river. It might go off somewheres if they didn't."

He laughed a dry, cackling laugh, and Coony jumped on his lap.

Nelly sat with her chin in her hand and stared out over the water.

Why hadn't she been born in a shanty boat, she wondered unhappily. She wouldn't have had to bother with all this business of being a lady. A shanty-boat girl could fight like a boy and nobody would think a thing of it. You never had to dress up; you could just lie around under the willows or on deck and eat and stay dirty and listen to old men like Grandpaw telling tales.

"That's a real purty dress you have on," the old man said presently. He took out a plug of tobacco and cut off a chunk. Tucking it into one cheek, he said, "Yeah, real purty."

"It was," said Nelly, "before I had a fight. Right on the church steps. My family is ashamed of me. I think I'll leave home so they'll never have to bother with me any more."

This sounded so sad that Nelly's chin quivered. Her eyes filling with tears, she turned away to hide them.

"Was it a good fight?' asked Grandpaw.

"Well, I licked him," said Nelly. "It was that Tom Broussard. He made fun of my hat . . ."

She had to tell Grandpaw about the hat, and then all her other troubles poured out—her problems with the cats, the long story of the frizzly chicken, and how her mother grieved because she was such a tomboy.

Grandpaw sat stroking Coony's tail and making little sounds of sympathy like "Pshaw!" "Tut-tut," and "Oh, fer pity sakes." But he let her talk until it was all out.

"I'm glad you come by," he said when Nelly had finished her story and had begun to feel a little better. "I've got somethin' fer you. Jest yestiddy somethin' come awalkin' up to this very door— somethin' I know you been lookin' fer. I got it round back. Come on!"

Something in his voice sent a wild rush of hope through Nelly. She practically walked on Grandpaw's heels as he pushed aside the willow branches and moved unsteadily around to the back of the shanty.

Under the overhanging trees was an old broken-down table and on the table was a box with a piece of fence wire stretched across the front. As Nelly went toward it a wonderful idea came into her head. But she brushed it aside because it was too wonderful to believe. It couldn't be—it just couldn't be—that Grandpaw had found a frizzly chicken!

"Take a peek in there," said Grandpaw.

Nelly leaned over. Huddled in one corner, looking as miserable as only a frizzly chicken can, was —sure enough—a frizzly.

"It's yourn," said Grandpaw. "I been savin' it fer ye."

"Where did you get it?" cried Nelly breathlessly.

"I didn't. The critter jest come walkin' in, and I recollected ye was wantin' one. So I jest put it up fer ye."

He reached inside the box and took out the chicken.

"Why it's mine!" cried Nelly. "It's the one I bought at Crawdad. See, it's got two little black feathers right on top of its head. It must've walked all this way."

"Lookin' fer ye," agreed Grandpaw, nodding. He

spit a long stream of tobacco juice into the willow brush. "And now he's found ye."

"Oh, Grandpaw!" cried Nelly, throwing her arms around him. "I can never, never, thank you! Oh, I'm so happy!"

"Hrumph—er—hrumph!" said Grandpaw, who didn't know what else to say. "Well, I'm real glad about that. Now ye take him an' git on home with him. Yer folks is likely worried to death about ye an' fit to be tied."

She ran almost all the way home. She went behind the houses, because she didn't want to be seen. She knew that she was so dirty that if any of her mother's friends saw her, they'd be shocked; and if any of the family saw her, it would cause an uproar. She wanted to get the frizzly safely to Rena before anything could happen to it or anyone could stop her.

Rena was on the back porch. She had just started to eat her dinner when she looked up and saw Nelly slipping through the back yard.

"Forevermore!" cried Rena, dropping her fork. "Will you tell me, please, where you been and what's happened to you?"

"Shhh!" warned Nelly. "I've been in a fight, and, look! I've got you a frizzly!"

Rena came slowly down the back steps and stood staring at Nelly. The little girl's face was red and streaked with perspiration, the Easter dress was dirty and had a snag in it, and the pink sash still trailed in the dust. In her arms the dirty chicken squawked and struggled.

"Who you take that away from?" asked Rena sternly.

"Nobody. I bought it . . . for you," said Nelly. "I didn't steal this one. I bought him. This is the one I bought in Crawdad."

"Now if that ain't the sweetest thing I ever knowed a child to do!" cried Rena, giving Nelly a hug that nearly smothered her.

"Look out, he'll get away!" cried Nelly. "Take him. I gotta go in and see Mamma."

Rena went off with the frizzly, talking to it as if it were a baby, and Nell walked slowly toward the house.

Suddenly a hissing sound came from the bushes along the fence. Nelly turned curiously and saw a tall good-looking boy with black curly hair looking over the bushes.

"I've been tryin' to find you," he said in a low tone. "Say! That was a swell beatin' you gave that smarty Tommy Broussard. He's my cousin and I hate him, but my mother won't let me touch him."

"Thanks," said Nelly. "My mother wouldn't have let me touch him either if she'd known about it. I reckon I was awful," she added, but she had to grin, thinking of Tom lying there in the road bellowing for help.

"You were great," said the boy, moving off. "And I'm sorry about your dress. Bye."

"Bye," said Nell and went into the house. She felt better in spite of having to face the family and not knowing what they would do to her. She *had* given that horrid boy a good beating, and she had replaced Rena's frizzly chicken. And that was a load off her shoulders.

She guessed she could stand what was coming to her about the fight. She walked into the house and found Missmamma and her mother in the parlor.

"Nelly," cried her mother, jumping up, "where have you been? Uncle Doctor and the boys are looking everywhere for you!"

"I went for a walk," said Nelly. "I—I reckoned you all wouldn't want me around. But I found a frizzly for Rena, so I came back. I'm sorry about the dress. But I'm glad I hit him," she added, with her eyes sparkling. "He was so hateful."

"Oh, Nelly!" cried her mother. "Go and get cleaned up. Rena has your dinner in the oven. Do you suppose you'll ever learn to behave like a lady?"

"I reckon so," said Nelly. "Anyway, I'll start trying. And you needn't buy me another hat until I've learned."

As Nelly went out Missmamma rose from her chair. "That child looks worn out," she said. "I'll go and see that she gets some milk and a good piece of that chocolate cake for dessert."

Nelly's Biggest Problem Is Solved

Rose and Callie and Nell sat in the porch swing, swaying lazily and eating bread-and-jelly sandwiches. The spring air was fresh and lovely, and all the world was green.

Under the pecan tree, which was in new full leaf and breaking into bloom, the gray-and-white cat lay surrounded by her kittens. They were not pretty, but they pranced and pounced and played as cutely as all kittens do. Nell tried not to see them from where she sat. She still hadn't found homes for them, and every few days her mother reminded her of it. Why didn't everybody like cats as much as she did, wondered Nelly.

Callie left the swing and began to hop around on one bare foot. "Here one, here anur," she sang. "Here two, top o 'tur. Here three wid laig all tied tergedder." It was an old selling song that the children had often heard in New Orleans and Natchez.

> Here's one, here's another,
> Here are two on top of each other,
> Here are three with their legs all tied together.

Uncle Doctor had explained that it was the way the Cajuns and other country people sold chickens, all at one price because it was easier than figuring out how much to charge for each chicken. They weighed up four pounds of chickens, say, and sold four pounds at a time, whether it took one, two, or three chickens.

Callie hopped and sang in a sleepy murmur.

"Here one, here anur. Here two——"

"Look!" cried Nelly suddenly. "There's a buggy coming down the road, and it looks like—but it can't be—*but it is!* It's Captain Jenkins and Mrs. Jenkins from the *Floating Palace!*"

No wonder Nelly looked astonished. The show-boat people had never been in Willow Landing at this time of year. What could it mean?

The girls got up and ran down to the road. The captain had stopped the buggy and gotten out. He turned to help Mrs. Jenkins, who waved at the children as she climbed down.

"Hello, landlubbers," said the captain. "I bet you're surprised to see us!"

"I should say so!" cried Nelly. "What are you doing here this time of year?"

"We've come to tell you good-bye," said Mrs. Jenkins. She put her arm around Nelly's shoulder as they walked toward the house. "We've had a terrible time!" she added. "The flood was much worse downriver. The river's deeper there, you know, and I guess it sort of gathers momentum as it comes down. Anyway, there was a lot of damage and our boat was broken up. Oh, nobody was hurt," she said quickly when the girls cried out in horror, "but the boat was so badly wrecked we've decided not to try to salvage it."

They went up on the porch, and Nell's mother came to meet them. She had to be told about the flood all over again.

"But what are you going to do?" she asked. "I can't imagine you not being on the showboat."

"We're going to England," said Mrs. Jenkins. "Matt's never seen where I came from or met any of my people. And then we're coming back here and travel."

"You know, the showboat business isn't what it used to be," said the captain. "Railroads are taking folks further inland, and towns are building theaters so that people don't have to come to the river for entertainment. We knew we'd have to quit before many years and when the *Floating Palace* busted up we thought it would be a good time to do it. We plan to open another kind of show later, but right now we're going to take it easy for a while."

"We won't see you—ever again?" cried Nelly.

"Oh, I'm sure you will!" said Mrs. Jenkins. "We'll be playing at Natchez later and maybe even here if Willow Landing ever grows big enough to have a stage. We're going to do real plays and have a stock company—after we've had a good vacation."

"Won't you stay for dinner?" asked Nell's mother as the captain rose.

"We'd like to, Ma'am," he answered, "but we've got to leave on the downriver boat. We're sailin' from New Orleans. But we just couldn't go without telling you folks good-bye. We stopped off to see Doc—we sure will miss seeing him every year—and we have some business to attend to."

The gray cat came to the top of the steps dragging one of her kittens, who was really too old to be carried.

"Matt!" said Mrs. Jenkins. "Look! Cats!"

Nelly could not imagine why Mrs. Jenkins was so amazed at the sight of an ordinary cat and kitten.

"Do you want to give some away?" asked the captain.

"She certainly does!" cried Miss Fanny. "We've been desperately trying to find homes for them. Don't you want a dozen or so?"

"We'll take all you have. You see, the flood broke up a number of barns and warehouses in the towns between here and New Orleans, and as a result the rats and mice are running all over the place. They came aboard boats and went into all the houses and stores that weren't flooded. Every place we went, they begged us for a cat."

"Will they be kind to them?" asked Nelly fearfully. It seemed a long way for her cats to go by themselves.

"They'll treasure them like the cats of Egypt," the captain assured her. "They'll be so glad to get them, they'll probably put up a monument to 'em!"

This sent Callie into giggles, and Miss Fanny said, "How could you take them . . . the cats, I mean?"

"We'll send the boys over with a cage," said Captain Jenkins. "We'll be very kind to them," he added. "But they'll have to be kept in something till we leave shore."

"Keep them in it until you are well down the river!" cried Miss Fanny. "All but one of the others that Nell gave away came home in less than a week!"

"You get them together," the captain told Nelly, "and we'll send the boys over to get them in about an hour."

"Don't grieve, Ducky," said Mrs. Jenkins, putting her arm around Nelly and giving her a big squeeze. "They'll live like kings. We had to give up Hanni-bal, you know. Couldn't take him all around the country with us. He's getting old, too, so we gave him to a man in New Orleans who runs a second-hand shop. You look for him when you go down there. The shop's on Bourbon Street. And won't it be fun when we meet again, maybe at a show in Natchez or Biloxi, and have a nice hot cuppa to-gether?"

Nelly tried not to cry, but Rose was fumbling for her handkerchief and Callie had gone back and was sitting on the steps, looking like a summer storm. Not to see the *Floating Palace* again, not to hear the calliope and see the wonders of the show itself, not to see the Jenkinses or Hannibal, and to lose the cats, too! It was a great deal to give up at one time.

The Jenkinses waved and called good-bye, the buggy started up in a spurt of dust, and they were gone.

"Now," cried Miss Fanny briskly, "you girls get the cats together. Aren't you glad they're going to have good homes, Nell? Try to think how nice it's going to be for them."

It wasn't easy. When Nell and her cousins went out to the barn the cats and their kittens came running.

"I feel awful!" said Nell mournfully. "They think I'm just going to feed them and I'm really getting ready to give them away."

"They won't care," said Callie. "Papa says all cats care about is their own comfort. Just so somebody feeds 'em, they don't much care who it is."

Nelly didn't believe it, not quite. But it made her feel a little better. After all, they would have good homes and be treated like kings—Mrs. Jenkins had said so. "We'll put 'em all in the feed bins till the Jenkins boys get here," she said.

So as each kitten finished its milk and began to wash its face, it was lifted gently, kissed tenderly, and dropped very carefully into one of the feed bins.

"Which ones are you going to keep?" asked Callie, pausing with the last of the gray cat's kittens in her arms.

"I'm only going to keep Rosalie," said Nell. "She'll have kittens again, maybe, and hers are so pretty."

The Jenkins boys appeared suddenly in the barn doorway. They carried a large wire cage with an old quilt on the floor of it.

"We'll spread 'em out in other cages later," said the older boy. "We're leaving on the *Andy Tucker,* and the captain wants a couple himself."

All too quickly the cats and kittens were caught and thrust into the cage. They seemed surprised but not unhappy. Nell and Callie and Rose walked out to the wagon with the Jenkins boys, saying, "Good-bye, Memphis Belle! Good-bye, River Queen! Good-bye, Magnolia! Good-bye! Good-bye!"

But things happened so quickly that the girls really didn't have time to mourn. Besides, Nell could not help being relieved that another one of her problems had been solved. She didn't know where on earth she could have given the cats away

in Willow Landing, and now they were all taken care of.

The double first cousins wandered off and Nell went back and sat on the steps under the pecan tree. Rosalie came and rolled over in the dust, holding her paws up in the air and rubbing her back into the dirt.

A small cloud of dust appeared on the big road, and a moment later a boy on a bicycle came hurtling along the road to the house. He stopped suddenly and jumped off, standing in front of Nell and wiping his hot face with a handkerchief. It was Tom Broussard's cousin, the tall boy who had hidden in the bushes to thank Nell for pounding Tom.

"Hi," he said.

Nell grinned. "Hi," she answered.

"Gosh, you look better now," said the boy, sitting down on the steps by her. "You're real pretty with your face clean."

The face in question turned a bright pink. Nell didn't know whether this was a compliment or not.

"My name's Sam Elliott. We moved here last month," said the boy. "I go to school at Jefferson. I'm just home for Easter vacation."

Nell said nothing. She wished Rose and Callie were here. It wasn't every day that a new boy—an older one—came to see them.

"I—me and my cousins—go to Miss Fink's," said Nell at last. "It's an awful school. There are only about ten of us, and we have to do an awful lot of work."

"You ought to go to Natchez to boarding school," said Sam. "Then you could go to the dances. The boys from Jefferson go down there to dances and things, and it's fun. I bet you can dance," he added.

"Not much," admitted Nell. "There's nobody but girls to dance with around here—girls and Bert, my cousin."

"Next time I'm home I'll teach you," said Sam

gallantly. "Then when you come to Natchez you'll be the belle of the ball. But you mustn't get into any fights," he added, laughing.

"Forget it," muttered Nell.

Sam laughed and picking up his bicycle, rode off. "See you when school's out," he called back.

Afterwards Nell sat on the steps, smiling to herself. He was a nice boy; she liked him. It was pleasant to look forward to seeing him in June. Maybe she would learn to dance and maybe she would go to Natchez. She and Rose and Callie couldn't go to Miss Fink's forever. By that time surely she would have learned to be a lady and her mother would buy her some more pretty clothes.

She had heard about the balls in Natchez. Her mother and aunts had gone to several of them. She began to dream about going—she and her cousins—and to picture what they would wear. She could just see Callie in pink chiffon. She would be lovely. "And I'll wear blue, pale blue, and Rose can wear a sort of creamy yellow; and I bet we *will* be the belles of the ball!" Maybe growing up and being a lady wouldn't be so bad after all.

Out in the kitchen Rena was singing one of the roustabout songs.

"De big wheel roll
And de head come 'round.
We's bound to go
Les' we take de ground.
Oh, Lordy! Lordy!"

When a steamboat "took de ground" it was stuck in one place and no good to anybody. Nelly thought that people were the same way. They couldn't stay in one place always. They, too, were "bound to go."

I guess goin' and growin' are sort of alike, she thought, picking up Rosalie, who had now brushed herself clean. I can't help growin' up, and maybe I'll like it after all. Anyway, I'm going to try.

Over on the river she heard the hoarse whistle of a steamboat. She put Rosalie down and went into the house, which was cool and dim and smelled of the strawberry jam Rena was making. She hadn't felt so happy in a long, long time.